Red Lips & White Lies

Tempting

USA TODAY BESTSELLING AUTHOR

BELLA MATTHEWS

TEMPTING

A KROYDON HILLS LEGACY NOVEL

RED LIPS & WHITE LIES
BOOK ONE

BELLA MATTHEWS

Editor: Dena Mastrogiovanni, Red Pen Editing

Cover Designer: Val, Books and Moods

Interior Formatting: Brianna Cooper

SENSITIVE CONTENT

This book contains sensitive content that could be triggering.
Please see my website for a full list.

WWW.AUTHORBELLAMATTHEWS.COM

This book is dedicated to my Momager, Brianna.
The woman who keeps my business running. Who drives five hours to ship out books.
Who stays on seventeen hour zoom calls to make sure the book gets done.
Thank you doesn't seem like enough for all that you do, so I figured I'd write you a book.

XOXO Bella.

"Time is precious. Make sure you spend it with the right people."

— UNKNOWN

CAST OF CHARACTERS

The Kings Of Kroydon Hills Family

- **Declan & Annabelle Sinclair**
  - Everly Sinclair - 28
  - Grace Sinclair - 28
  - Nixon Sinclair - 27
  - Leo Sinclair - 26
  - Hendrix Sinclair - 23

- **Brady & Nattie Ryan**
  - Noah Ryan - 25
  - Lilah Ryan - 25
  - Dillan Ryan - 22
  - Asher Ryan - 16

- **Aiden & Sabrina Murphy**
  - Jameson Murphy -25
  - Finn Murphy - 22

- **Bash & Lenny Beneventi**
  - Maverick Beneventi - 25
  - Ryker Beneventi - 23

- **Cooper & Carys Sinclair**
  - Lincoln Sinclair - 18
  - Lochlan Sinclair - 18
  - Lexie Sinclair - 18

- **Coach Joe & Katherine Sinclair**
  - Callen Sinclair - 28

The Kingston Family

- **Ashlyn & Brandon Dixon**
  - Madeline Kingston - 29
  - Raven Dixon - 13

- **Max & Daphne Kingston**
  - Serena Kingston - 22

- **Scarlet & Cade St. James**
  - Brynlee St. James - 28
  - Killian St. James - 26
  - Olivia St. James - 24

- **Becket & Juliette Kingston**
  - Easton Hayes - 33
  - Kenzie Hayes - 27
  - Blaise Kingston - 17

- **Sawyer & Wren Kingston**
  - Knox Kingston - 21
  - Crew Kingston - 18

- **Hudson & Maddie Kingston**
  - Teagan Kingston - 22
  - Aurora Kingston - 19
  - Brooklyn Kingston - 14

- **Amelia & Sam Beneventi**
  - Maddox Beneventi - 27
  - Caitlin Beneventi - 24
  - Roman Beneventi - 22

- o Lucky Beneventi - 20

- **Lenny & Bash Beneventi**
  - o Maverick Beneventi - 25
  - o Ryker Beneventi - 23

- **Jace & India Kingston**
  - o Cohen Kingston - 21
  - o Saylor Kingston - 16
  - o Atlas Kingston - 13
  - o Asher Kingston - 13

For family trees, please visit my website
www.authorbellamatthews.com

Can't put my finger on what I'm in the mood for . . . Could be tacos and a margarita. A little online shopping? Maybe an orgasm . . . *Yup*. That's it. Ding-ding-ding! Orgasm is the winner.

—*Kenzie's Secret Thoughts*

*C*oming home is a strange thing—especially after four years.

You *think* everything will be the same, and in a lot of ways, it is . . . but *different.*

Life has a sneaky way of doing that when you're least expecting it.

Changing. Whether you want it to or not.

The last time I was in West End was the night before I moved to Washington, DC, for my ob-gyn residency. It was only four years ago, but it feels like a lifetime. The bar's vibe is a mix between industrial and craftsman. Exposed wood beams and wide-planked reclaimed wood floors and tables are warmed by Edison bulbs strung overhead, while black metal chairs and stools scattered throughout manage to somehow balance the warmth with a cool, edgy feel that's so perfectly fitting for the owner. The atmosphere is casually cool, and the food is delicious.

It's been one of the town's favorite hot spots since my cousin Maddox opened it years ago, and tonight is no exception. The place is packed, and our motley crew of friends and family take up an entire corner of the room. Not surprising, since we've always traveled in packs.

Where there's one, there's usually many, and tonight, we're at least twenty deep. Football season is in full swing, and hockey preseason officially starts next week, meaning this will be one of the last times we get this many of the guys together at once for a little while. That's probably why everyone seems so carefree tonight. Jokes are flying, and beer is flowing.

Everyone is enjoying themselves.

Everyone except Maddox, that is.

Carefree is rarely a word I'd use to describe my cousin.

Asshole, occasionally. Sarcastic, always. Carefree . . . not really.

He hands me a glass of water with a lemon wedge and arches one dark, bushy eyebrow like a cartoon villain. "Better make sure you don't drink too many of these. We wouldn't want you to loosen up and lose control tonight."

Yup. Still a sarcastic fucker.

I know how to lose control.

"Whatever, shithead. I'm on call as of midnight tonight." I drop my lemon into the glass, then push it down with the straw. "Booze and babies don't mix."

"Not unless you're making them," he argues with a smirk before moving further down the bar to grab an order from a woman twice his age who's looking at him like *he* might be on the menu.

Apparently not *everything* changes.

My cousin Brynlee grabs my hand and presses it against her baby bump to feel her baby boy going to town on her ribcage. "Can't you deliver him now?" she pouts.

"Nope. You've got four more weeks, Brynnie. You're a rockstar. You've got this." I dig my fist into the small of her back, alleviating some of the pressure this little man has been putting on his momma, and she drops her head and moans in relief.

"God, I love you. How about you come home with us? I'll kick Deacon out of bed. You can have his spot."

Like a homing beacon, her hot, hockey-coach giant of a husband hears his name and zeroes in on his wife. "You kicking me out of bed, red?"

"Depends . . . Can you do what she just did?" she challenges, and the smile splashing across Deacon's face is filthy, which has me quickly looking away.

It's been so damn long since someone looked at me with filthy thoughts dancing behind their eyes. At least any *someones* I want looking at me that way.

"Get your mind out of the gutter, Coach," Brynn giggles, and I take that as my cue to slide away before I hear something I don't want or need to know.

My friends have no boundaries or filters.

I love them. Truly I do. Even if they put the *Sex and the City* ladies to shame with the way they all love to talk about their sex lives. Samantha would be proud. Maybe if I had a sex life, I wouldn't be as over the constant talk as I am. But man . . . when you're the only one not having hot sex—sex with a professional athlete, no less—let alone, the only one who's never had an orgasm provided by something that doesn't require a charging cord, it gets a little old.

Even Charlotte got laid on the old show, and I'm not as uptight as she was.

"I'd like to make a toast." My big brother, Easton, tugs me

to his side and raises his beer. "To my baby sister, Mackenzie. Congratulations on your new job, Kenz. It's good to finally have you home." Everyone raises their drinks high in the air and cheers. "Love you, kid."

He drops a kiss on the top of my head like I'm one of his babies instead of his sister.

"Dude. She's two years younger than your wife. Not sure I'd be calling her *kid*," one of the guys, I think Callen, laughs, and Easton flips him off before I wiggle out of his hold.

"Maybe they're into that," gets called out before Lindy shakes her head and kisses Easton's cheek. She whispers something in his ear, and he smacks her ass.

I'm surrounded by hornballs.

All of them.

But even that thought puts a smile on my face because they're my people.

And it's hard to put into words how much I've missed being with them.

My friends.

My *family*.

The ones I claimed as my own after our mom died and left Easton and me with our cousin Juliette as our legal guardian. Jules married Becket Kingston and managed to give us an enormous family who took us in and claimed us as their own. But even better, with them came Brynlee and Lindy. The closest thing I'd ever had to sisters. They introduced me to the twins, Everly and Grace, and as they say, *the rest is history.* My history.

These women took in a heartbroken little girl and refused to let me close myself off.

We were inseparable.

The kind of girl squad most teenage girls—hell, most grown women—dream of.

The kind that cheers the loudest for you, even if you're not around to hear it.

Who protects your name in rooms you're not in.

Friends who make sure—even though you're going through your residency, hours away, working eighty-hour weeks with no time off to come home—you're still in every text thread and on as many FaceTimes as possible. They made sure I didn't miss a thing, even if I couldn't be here to watch it happen in person.

Even Callen and Maddox texted and sent funny memes.

Completely inappropriate ones that made me laugh so hard I cried.

My honorary brothers.

Of course, Lindy went and married my actual brother, and now I'm stuck hearing about their sex life whenever she feels like torturing me, which is often. But I did get the cutest niece and nephew out of it, so I'll deal.

Like I said . . . *same, but different.*

"You're awful quiet over here, Mac."

I look up through my lashes at the twins' brother, Nixon, wondering when he got hot. I guess that's another one of those new things. I don't remember Nix being quite so . . . broad. He was always the quieter Sinclair sibling. The one who went away to Boston for college and came back right before I left for Washington, DC.

His younger brother Leo leans back against the bar on my other side, grinning like a goof. "So, Kenz. You seriously get to look at vaginas all day? Don't you get sick of 'em? Don't get me wrong, I love me some—"

"Leo—" Gracie turns to her brother with fire burning in her eyes as she stops his verbal vomit. "Do not finish that sentence."

"But—" he starts, and she yanks his earlobe like a naughty

child and tugs him away, muttering something about manners.

Nixon shakes his head as he tries unsuccessfully to stifle his laugh. "You think your brother is gonna stop toasting the fact you're home any time soon? Pretty sure this is at least the third time since you got back in town."

"Probably not," I admit sheepishly and glance over at Easton. Lindy's arms are wrapped around his waist as she laughs at something someone just said. Easton's relaxed and smiling, and it makes my heart so freaking happy. He spent a long damn time not smiling, and I'll love my best friend forever for giving him the kind of peace she brings to his life.

When I drag my eyes back to Nix, he taps his bottle of beer to my glass with a wicked grin on his handsome face. "To you being home, Mac."

"Thanks, Nix." I try unsuccessfully to stifle a yawn, then cover my mouth, mortified.

"Oh, I see how it is," he teases.

"Stop." My cheeks burn red. "I'm on call in a few hours, and it's a full moon. I should probably go try to catch a little sleep while I still can." I look around, hoping no one is paying me any attention so I can make my escape without any guilt trips stopping me.

Nixon crosses well-defined arms over his chest, blocking me from everyone's view, and I wonder when exactly they got so *thick* too.

I've known him since we were twelve, and Nixon Sinclair never used to be . . . well . . . *hot.*

He was always a good-looking guy. Tall, dark, and handsome, just like his dad. But kind of quiet, a little awkward, and always obsessed with hockey. You never really saw Nix with a girlfriend. He was always surrounded by the Kroydon Hills Prep's hockey team in high school. He didn't party much. If you needed him, you could usually find him on the ice somewhere.

But somewhere between then and now, Nixon grew into a *seventh circle of Hell* hot man.

When exactly did that happen, and how exactly did I miss it?

My eyes trail over his chest and down his arms, stopping on the muscles there long enough to decide the temptation is too good to resist. I squeeze one of the biceps currently testing the strength of the dark gray cotton t-shirt covering his tanned, obviously toned chest and bite down on my bottom lip, hiding my smile. "You know steroids cause erectile disfunction, right, Nix?"

"Jesus Christ, Mackenzie," he chuckles. "I'm not taking steroids."

When I quietly cock my head to the side, he laughs harder. "I'd get kicked out of the league."

I drag my eyes over him one more time and shrug. "Just saying . . . it would be a shame to destroy a perfectly good body."

"Perfect body, huh?" he counters with a sexy smile, and I force myself to ignore the way his lips tip up at one corner.

You do not flirt with your best friends' brother.

Girl code . . . or something like that.

At least that's the excuse I'm sticking with.

"That's the only part you heard?" I chew my lip with a shake of my head and remind myself that he not only is my best friends' brother but a professional hockey player too. This man is most likely a player in every possible aspect, not to mention so far beyond the tiny bit of lackluster experience I've got, he should be in a whole other stratosphere.

"Whatever . . ." I shake away that train of thought before it turns into an entire runaway locomotive. "If anyone asks, can you let them know I'm heading home?"

"You walking?" he asks as he pulls out his wallet and drops a handful of bills on the bar.

"We live four streets away from here, Nix. It's not like I was going to drive." It's also not like Kroydon Hills is known for its high crime rate. Walking was a no-brainer.

When my residency ended, I had no intention of moving back into the building the girls and I all lived in after college. Not because it wasn't a great place to live. The condos are beautiful with big open floor plans, nice bathrooms, and state of the art kitchens. One I'll probably never use, but that's beside the point. Of course, my family owns the damn building. Half my cousins live there. And the few tenants I'm not related to are related to the twins, like Callen, Nixon, and Leo. And every single one of them is nosey as hell. This town makes *Gossip Girl* look like *Sesame Street* in comparison. Gossip might as well be its main export after professional athletes.

I guess I've gotten used to having my own space, and a little bit of privacy goes a long way. Especially since I work insane hours. It's not like babies are born on schedules, and I'm padding my resume with as much experience as possible. I've been toying with the idea of applying for a fellowship, and the hours look great on an application.

When I come home, I don't want to worry about who I run into and what they'll say. And my friends are everywhere. I've already come home twice to Callen raiding my fridge and woke up once to Maddox having a cup of coffee in my kitchen. Lucky for him, he brought me one too, so I let him live instead of practicing my scalpel skills on him like a fresh cadaver.

And . . . it's barely been two weeks since I moved back in.

I've already reached out to a realtor to see if I can find a little house to rent for now until I'm ready to buy something more permanent.

Nixon follows me through the bar, then tugs on my elbow to stop near his brother. The Sinclair genes are strong, and Leo and Nixon are both so similar. But where Nix is tall, dark, and handsome, Leo looks more like the twins with surfer-boy good looks, even if they're on the body of one of the fastest guys in professional hockey. "Hey, man, I'm walking Mac home. Catch up later."

Leo nods and goes back to the women he was talking to.

"I can walk four blocks alone, Nixon," I protest as he opens the door of West End and waits for me to walk through.

"Just because you *can* doesn't mean you *should*," he argues, and I resist the eye roll that's coming. "I don't remember you being this stubborn, Mac."

"Yeah well, I don't remember you being this bossy, Nix." A weird little zing of electricity passes between us as I brush by him and almost fall flat on my face. I catch myself as I trip over the metal door frame. Stupid heels. They make my legs and ass look incredible in this dress, but they pinch the shit out of my toes.

Guess I'm paying the price now.

Nixon's hands reach out and right me, making sure I don't fall.

Yup. There's that little zing again.

What the hell is up with that?

He doesn't drop his hands right away as the front door swings shut behind us, and a throat clears in front of us.

One that sends an unwelcome awareness down my spine.

"Dr. Hayes," the unwelcome voice cuts into the building tension.

Nixon must sense my unease because instead of letting go, he tugs me closer to him, and I watch Dr. Dick's eyes track the movement.

"Dr. Richardson," I answer *professionally*. Not that I have a choice. He's the head of Obstetrics and Gynecology at Kroydon Hills Hospital. And since the practice I now work for delivers most of their babies there, I'll be dealing with this man often.

Dr. Dick, as I overheard a few nurses refer to him quietly last week, stands in front of us in pressed khakis and a polo, easily in his mid-forties and kind of hot in an all-American sort of way, but also kind of creepy in a pushy, uncomfortable, might not take no for an answer, sort of way too. Dr. Dick asked me out during my very first day of rounds at the hospital, and I politely declined. I have no desire to date one of my bosses, let alone someone whose ego proceeds him.

He hasn't quite accepted my *no, thank-you* though.

I've ignored his overt flirting, refusing to acknowledge it.

That's not how I want to start my career.

There's something about him I can't quite place my finger on.

He towers over me, but next to Nixon, he looks small. And he's absolutely sizing Nixon up when his eyes get caught on the big hand wrapped around my waist, resting tightly on my hip.

Yeah . . . I want to tell him it's distracting the hell out of me too.

"I wasn't aware you were seeing someone, Mackenzie."

Okay, so my go-to answer right now should probably be, *why the hell would you be aware?* We're not friends, and I don't talk about my personal life . . . or lack thereof.

Like. Ever.

Becket Kingston, the closest thing I'll ever have to a father, is a very high-profile Senator, so I learned early on to keep my private life just that . . . *private*. I don't bother with social media. I don't talk about my family or my famous friends outside my circle. And this man is not my friend.

Not that any of that actually matters because I'm not seeing Nixon Sinclair.

Hell . . . I haven't been *seeing someone* since high school.

But as Nixon's grip tightens on my hip, I'm not sure anyone told him that.

Nixon

Chapter 2

I've got a bad fucking feeling about this douche.

I don't know who he is, but I don't like him or the way he's looking at Mac.

She tensed up the minute she saw him, and that's all I need to know. A woman doesn't tense up unless you've done something incredibly right or significantly wrong. And it doesn't seem like this dude has done anything right.

This woman is my sisters' best friend, which makes her part of my circle.

And I protect what's mine.

Mackenzie moves the slightest bit closer to me. Her long, soft chestnut-brown hair blows in the wind, causing the gentle scent of spicy vanilla sugar to invade my senses, and my mouth waters as every protective instinct my father drilled into my brothers and me all our lives kicks into overdrive.

My grip on her hip tightens, firmer than I mean for it to be, while I reach out to him with my other hand. "Don't you want to introduce me, Mac?"

My words sound almost threatening, and I don't bother tempering them.

Let him be threatened.

Mackenzie looks up through long, inky-black lashes and worries her pouty bottom lip before forcing a small, fake as fuck smile. "Nixon, this is Dr. Richardson. He's head of my department at the hospital."

Dr. Richardson looks like an uptight, entitled prick who belongs on a polo horse. If that weren't an insult to the horse. He glances disdainfully from her to me before tentatively offering me his hand in a limp-ass handshake.

Fucking pussy.

He winces when I squeeze more forcefully than necessary.

Probably because I'm a dick who just made sure he knows which of us would win in a fight. Maybe he'll take it as the warning it's meant to be not to fuck with a woman half his size. Especially this one. Mackenzie is barely five-five and might be a hundred and ten pounds soaking wet.

My mind drifts to her standing in the shower. Her damp hair hanging down around her shoulders. Bubbles lathered on her wet skin . . .

Fuck—that's a pretty fucking picture.

When I grin, he rips his hand away, like he knows what I just saw in my mind, and wipes his palm on his starched khakis like he just touched dog shit. "Zane Richardson. And you are . . . ?"

Kenzie takes another small step into my side, and that bad fucking feeling grows.

Guess that's going to be my excuse for what I'm about to do.

Couldn't have anything to do with the fact that this girl was the first girl I ever crushed on before I even knew all the ways I wanted to make her scream my fucking name. What can I say? We were thirteen, and she was the new girl in a bikini in my parents' pool. She was a literal wet dream come to life.

And there goes that picture of her in the shower again.

"Nixon Sinclair." I let my glare go dark like it does before a fight on the ice. "Her boyfriend."

Mac's breath gets stuck in her chest before she lifts those shock-filled, honey-brown eyes my way. After a minute, her surprise turns into a small, hesitant smile—still fake, but not as obvious this time—when she turns back to this asshole.

Dr. Richardson nods slowly. Creepy as fuck. A little too calculated for my liking. "Sinclair . . . Your name sounds familiar," he muses as if trying to place me.

Good luck, asshole. There's a shit ton of Sinclairs in this town, and I'm related to all of them.

"Nixon plays for the Revolution with my brother," Kenzie offers sweetly, her voice quiet. Too quiet for this woman.

"Hockey?" he says the word like it's beneath him, and I grind my teeth. "For some reason, I was thinking football."

"That's my father and grandfather," I grunt and wait for it to click.

I don't have to wait long.

"Your dad is Declan Sinclair? The hall of fame quarterback for the Philly Kings?" he asks with an awe in his voice I know well. Declan Sinclair is pretty fucking awe-inspiring. He's a pretty amazing dad too. "That makes your grandfather the coach."

I nod, used to this shit.

This town worships football, and my family *is* Philly football.

Dad. Grandpa. Uncles. Cousins.

Poor Dad got three hockey-player sons instead of football players though.

We like to say we're tougher.

Anyone can throw a ball.

But can they do it on a blade less than three inches thick, skating backward?

These are the arguments we have over Thanksgiving dinner.

And maybe every other meal we eat together.

"Well then, I guess I'll be seeing you two at the gala next week. I believe your mother is one of the chairs of the event, Mr. Sinclair."

I look to Kenzie, not knowing what gala he's talking about but not willing to let him in on that fact.

Her tongue darts out and wets her lips, and I might be going to hell because I really shouldn't be picturing what those lips would look like wrapped around my dick . . . but I sure as shit am.

Fuck me.

What is it about this tiny woman that's always made my mind spin in ways it shouldn't?

She plays into my ruse and laces her fingers with mine. "I think we were waiting to see what your preseason schedule looks like."

"When did you say it was?" I ask, almost forgetting fuck-face next to us until he decides to insert himself back into our conversation.

"It's next Saturday at the Kroydon Hills Plaza Hotel. We're raising money for the hospital's autism research department," this asshole tells me.

Now that makes sense. My uncle has autism, and Mom has always championed research and resources for neurodivergent kids in Kroydon Hills. Guess I'm going to a gala.

"But I'm sure Kenzie can manage without you, Mr. Sinclair."

The way he says her name, like she's an expensive toy he's been denied . . . I don't like it.

"Mackenzie *would* be fine without me," I confirm because

this woman is more than capable of taking care of herself. "But she won't need to be. My first preseason game isn't until the following week. I'll be escorting her."

"Oh, Nix. You don't have to—"

I squeeze her hand, and she purses her lips before she can finish her sentence.

"I think it's time we get you to bed, Mac." Okay, so yeah, I'm a dick, and I know exactly what that sounded like, but I don't like this asshole. I don't like the way he's looking at her, and maybe I *do* like the way she's looking at me. "You wanted to catch a few hours of sleep before you're on call."

Richardson nods slowly. "I'll see you at the hospital then, Dr. Hayes."

He's trying to act unaffected but failing.

"Yes. I'll see you later," she tells him as I tug her in front of me. Kenzie rolls her eyes as we walk away. Guess I'm not the only one reverting to their teenage selves. "You know you're terrible, right?" she hisses.

"Listen, he already thinks I'm your boyfriend. Nothing wrong with him thinking I'm putting you to bed. I am a gentleman, after all." I will also not be going anywhere near her bed. Not for my own sanity. A man has his limits, and I'm already pushing mine.

She smacks my shoulder with her tiny purse and smiles her first real smile since we walked outside. One that has a tiny dimple appearing in her right cheek in the middle of a pretty pink flush that creeps up her creamy skin. I may not have spent much time with this woman since we graduated from high school, but some things you don't forget. And that smile is one of them.

"What was with that anyway? The whole *I'm her boyfriend* thing?" Her words are whispered, like the asshole can still hear us.

"Wanna tell me why you're scared of him?" I walk in front of her, then turn to face her and walk backward, wanting to see her reaction.

"Scared? Of Dr. Dick?" she scrunches her nose.

"Dr. Dick?" I ask, laughing as it dawns on me . . . *Richardson . . . Dick.* "Dr. Dick. That's perfect for that douche."

Kenzie's shoe gets caught in the sidewalk, and she jerks forward *again* and grasps the front of my shirt to stop her fall.

"Still a klutz, Mac? That's twice."

She looks down instead of meeting my eyes. "Still calling me Mac, Nix?"

"Pretty sure I've never called you anything else." I haven't.

Not since the first time my sisters brought her home.

"Whatever," she mumbles, then shoves me back. "I wasn't thinking about walking home when I picked out my shoes earlier."

I stop and turn around, giving her my back, and squat down. "Hop on."

"What?" she laughs.

"Hop on. I'll carry you." I look over my shoulder and catch her chewing that bottom lip again. "Come on, Mac. You can't walk home barefoot, and you've almost kissed the ground twice since you left the bar. It's not like it's your first piggyback ride." *Jesus.* She brings out the inner thirteen-year-old in me.

"I'm wearing a dress, Nix." Her protest is weak at best, and I can tell she's thinking about it.

"Come on, Mac. Hitch up your damn dress and hop on. I bench press four times your weight. We'll be home in five minutes, and you won't break your ankle between now and then."

She looks up at the twinkly-light-lined trees before

huffing and placing the skinny strap of her purse across her chest. "Fine. But if you tell anyone I did this, I'll kill you. I'm a doctor, Nixon. Don't think I can't do it. I can, and I can make it look like an accident."

That threat should probably scare me, but instead, I laugh. This woman used to capture spiders and set them free in the backyard when my sisters screamed. "Consider me warned, doc."

She climbs on and locks her knees in at my waist, and yeah . . . I need to get my mind out of the gutter.

I adjust her and try to ignore the feel of her soft skin and the way I wonder if it would taste like sugar on my tongue.

Doctor or not, this woman might be more dangerous than I thought.

Kenzie

Our doorman tries to hide the sideways look he gives Nix and me but fails as Nixon walks right past him with his hands anchored through my knees, absolutely refusing to put me down. The ankle strap of my hot-pink patent-leather stilettos dangle from my fingertips, and I wonder what we must look like. "Oh my goodness, Nixon. Put me down before someone else sees."

But does he listen?

No.

He hoists me further up his back and chuckles instead. "Wouldn't want a scandal, now would we, Mac?"

We pass the dark coffee shop which closed hours ago before stopping at the elevator. He swings me around so I can press the up button, keeping his grip tight the entire time.

The shiny doors open with their dramatic chime, and Nixon walks through like he's done this a thousand times. And I guess as far as I know, maybe he has. He's a professional hockey player. I know what the puck bunnies are like, and I'm just going to ignore the fact I just compared myself to a one. Damn it . . . I am so over this night.

It only takes a few moments before the doors open onto our floor, and we step out because—as if this night hasn't been humiliating enough—Nixon is basically forced to walk me to my front door since we're the only two condos on this floor.

"Here you go." He slides me down and off his back, and I ignore the way his muscles bunch under my touch. That is a whole lot of muscle. "You're home and in one piece." Nixon's eyes trail down over my face to my dangling pink shoes. "Might want to retire those though. Pretty sure I saved you twice tonight." Then that damn smirk comes back out to play again. "Three times, if you count Dr. Dick."

"Oh. My. God," I gasp, forgetting that I was about to yell at him for insinuating I should chuck my favorite heels . . . even if he's right. "You can't call him that to his face, Nix." I don't mention that I, along with half the staff, call him that behind his back. "You know you don't really have to come to the gala with me. If he asks, I'll tell him we're just friends. I'm not sure why you did that."

Nix shrugs. "I didn't like the way he was talking to you. The guy set my Spidey senses off. Besides, it will make my momma happy if I go to the gala, and now I have a reason to go. What time am I picking you up?"

"You're Spidey senses? You really should get that looked at, Nixon." I put my key in the lock and smile back at him.

Almost flirting . . . almost.

Because I don't flirt.

I'm not really sure I'd even know how. And I certainly wouldn't know how to do *it*, or anything else, with this man. "They can probably prescribe you something for that."

His hand covers mine on the knob, stopping me. "What time, Mac?"

Oh. Joking Nixon is fun, but bossy Nixon just dropped his voice into a no-nonsense gravelly octave that may have sent a shiver down my spine.

"It starts at seven," I answer quietly before firming up my voice. "Honestly, Nixon. I don't need you to go. I don't want to lie to everyone about having a boyfriend." A flush of embarrassment blooms in my cheeks, and something tightens in my chest because I wouldn't have a clue what to do with one of those either.

Nix drops his hand from mine and takes a step back. "We don't have to lie to anyone but Dr. Dick. If anyone else asks, we're two friends going to the same gala. So why not go together? Besides, I already donate to my mom's autism charity. If she's raising money for the hospital's department, it's a good cause."

"Nixon—" I try to stop him, but my words die on my tongue with his devious smile.

"See you next Saturday at six forty-five, Mac. Now go inside so I can go to bed."

"What?" I ask, utterly confused, but Nixon ignores the confusion and looks from me to the door.

"Go inside and lock the door so I can go to bed, Mackenzie," he tells me in that same gravelly voice, and I'm pretty sure he's serious.

"You're not my babysitter, Nixon," I warn him even as I take a step inside and leave my hand on the door.

"Nope. But I am your fake boyfriend, Mac. Now shut the

damn door and lock it." His baby-blue eyes crinkle in the corners as one side of his lips tip up in a sexy, nearly predatory grin, and I suddenly wonder what I've gotten myself into.

Guess we're going to find out.

Kenzie

Chapter 3

**I might not be able to find the words to explain how I feel,
but you can bet your sweet ass I'll find a song that can.**

—Kenzie's Secret Thoughts

ime always seems to move at two speeds, warp or slower than a snail, and the following week is no exception. My hours are insane. The cases run the gamut of textbook births to a fifty-six-year-old woman wanting to be a surrogate for her daughter, and everything in between. And I fucking love it. I'm here for it all and I'm grateful every day that I get to do this job and get paid to do what I love.

But some days . . . some days, when the exhaustion is running high and the sleep is at a minimum, I still question my sanity. Today is definitely leaning toward one of those days.

I drop my face into my hands and take a few deep breaths before my momentary silence is interrupted by the scraping of a cafeteria chair against the old linoleum floor like nails on a chalkboard, forcing me to look up too soon.

"Hey . . ." my friend Bellamy groans, much less peppy than

her usually cheerful self as she sits down across from me, a chocolate chip cookie in hand that she breaks in half before handing me a piece. Her dark hair is falling out of the space buns sitting on top of her head, and her formerly light-blue nurse's scrubs look a little worse for wear as she kicks her crocs up on the chair across from her. "What are you still doing here? I thought you got off an hour ago?"

"Last patient was a rough delivery." I don't tell her how rough because nobody needs to hear that. "How about you? You look like you need a shower and about seventy-two hours of sleep," I muse as I pop a piece of cookie in my mouth. Pretty sure this is the first thing I've eaten in hours. Nothing like a stale cookie and burned coffee for breakfast at eleven a.m. after skipping dinner the previous night.

Bellamy slid easily into our friend group once her oldest brother married Everly, but truthfully, she'd already been on the fringes without us knowing it. She's one of the few women who adores my cousin Caitlin. Maddox's little sister can be a bit much, but she and Bellamy have been best friends and roommates for years. She's also one of the few people I knew here at the hospital when I started working at my aunt Wren's ob-gyn practice and delivering babies here.

"Listen, I've been on for eighteen hours straight because the flu is hitting early, and four nurses called out. And that was after working three twelves already this week." She looks down at her shirt, then sniffs a spot and cringes. "I need to do laundry. I need a shower. And I need to eat something that wasn't made in this cafeteria. Not necessarily in that order. But for now, I'll settle for a shower and my bed. How about you?"

I shake my head slowly. "I've got to stop by Everly's shop before I can go to bed. I promised Wren I'd go to the gala the hospital is throwing this weekend and represent the practice.

She's out of town visiting her son's college for his game this weekend."

"Here." Bellamy's face falls, and she places the rest of the cookie on a napkin next to my coffee. "Sounds like you might need this more than I do."

"Guess that means I won't be seeing you at the event?" I ask, jealous and not at all looking forward to Saturday night or the complications I'm already envisioning.

"Nope. I'm working another twelve that night. But it's been the buzz of the hospital all week. Do you have a date for it? I think my brothers and Everly and Grace are going."

My cheeks heat.

Great. That's just what I need.

The twins to already be at the event when I show up with their little brother.

They always call all their brothers their *little brothers*, even if Nixon is nearly a foot taller and only a year younger than them. I think it was their way of torturing him, especially since he was physically bigger than both girls before he even hit puberty.

"What's up with that look?" Bellamy's eyes narrow as she points at my cheeks. "Do you have an actual date? Like a *guy* date?"

I tip my head to the side and roll my lips together, unsure how to answer.

"Mackenzie . . . is he a *hot guy* date?" Her smile grows slowly as she waits, but once she decides she's waited long enough, she snatches her cookie back. "No chocolate for you, if you're getting laid and keeping it secret."

I open my mouth to correct her but laugh instead when she pops a piece in her mouth and points again, this time with the cookie. "Chocolate is reserved for those of us that need the extra help with endorphins . . . *like me*. I don't remember the last time I got laid by something that doesn't require batteries."

I take my time and swallow the remnants of my crappy coffee in my paper cup before looking at my friend. "First, you need to get a vibrator with a charging cord. Take it from someone who knows. Total game changer." Bellamy opens her mouth to interrupt, but I put my finger up. "Nope. Still my turn."

Her smile grows to almost cartoon-like proportions, like she thinks she's about to get all the juicy gossip.

Poor thing obviously doesn't know me as well as she must think she does if she's expecting me to have dirty details to share.

Hell . . . I'd settle for remembering what dirty details actually feel like.

And on that note, I point my finger right at Bellamy. "Now, *second*, I'm right there with you, sister. I do have a date. But it's a pity date." And with that thought, I toss the rest of the cookie into my mouth and wish it was at least a Sweet Temptations cookie and not a dried-out, three-day-old one from the cafeteria. Chocolate really does release endorphins, but all this one does is make me wish I had a cup of milk to wash down the dry crumbs.

Bellamy waits a minute, then raises her hand.

"Oh my God, what?" I laugh and gently smack her hand down.

"Explain pity date," she demands.

I look around at the crowded cafeteria. There aren't any workers near us, just a few people chatting two tables away. "Dr. Dick sort of cornered me the other night when I left West End. Nixon and I were walking home, and he assumed Nix was my boyfriend."

Her eyebrows shoot up so high they nearly touch her hairline. "Why would he assume that?"

I shake my head and look around again, frustrated to even be having this conversation. There isn't a snowball's chance in hell I want anyone else to hear this. "I don't know. I tripped. Nixon caught me, and Dr. Dick apparently saw it. He made an assumption, and instead of correcting him, Nixon played into it," I whisper-hiss the last few words, still wondering why I agreed to this crazy plan. But Bellamy doesn't seem surprised. "Why don't you look shocked?"

She reaches up and yanks her rubber band off her hair, then runs her fingers through it before re-doing her messy bun.

Definitely a nervous habit, if I've ever seen one.

"Listen. I lived with Nixon for a few months before Caitlin and I moved in with her brother and the guys. Nix is a good guy with a protective streak a mile wide. It's just who he is. And I can only imagine the vibes he was catching off Dr. Dick. That asshole gives me the heebie-jeebies on a good day. And I haven't seen him have too many good days since I started working here."

"What's his deal?" I ask, honestly curious. I was lucky. After I finished my residency in DC, I came back to Kroydon Hills and stepped right into my aunt's ob-gyn practice. She welcomed me with open arms, and the last thing I want to do is sound like I'm complaining to her, so I've kept my thoughts on Dr. Dick to myself.

"He's just another handsy doctor. We've got a few of them, to be honest. Most of us just ignore him. He's the head of the department. He's triple board-certified and can perform surgeries less than ten doctors in this country are qualified to perform. Who do you think the hospital values more? Him or us?" she asks, already resigned to her answer.

That's what I thought, but it doesn't make it right.

"I get it. I'm not his biggest fan either, and Nixon could tell. So he said he was my boyfriend, then lied and said he's taking me to the gala." I drop my face back into my hands, knowing I'm going to have to tell his sisters this too. "Anyway. It's this weekend, and Everly said she has a dress for me. I'm stopping there on my way home to pick it up."

"Nixon Sinclair is sex on a stick, Kenz. Maybe he could help you with those rechargeable needs." She grins as we both stand from the table and gather our trash in our hands. "I bet he could go all night long."

"Whatever . . ." I shake my head and toss my trash in the bin. "It's not like I'm going to be finding that out."

$\mathcal{L}$ater that day, I look at my reflection in the three mirrors angled toward me as I stand on the dais in Everly's flagship store. She and Lindy opened Everly Wilder Designs a few years ago. It was originally just couture wedding gowns designed by Everly and managed by Lindy. Since then, they've brought a few employees on, including the addition of Caitlin as a junior designer. She focuses on bespoke tuxedos, bridal party dresses, evening gowns, and cocktail dresses. She has her hands in them all.

All three women look at me with varying shades of amusement when I finish explaining my fake-a-date predicament for Saturday while Caitlin pins the hem of the beautiful pink silk dress that's currently hitting me somewhere between ankle and mid-calf. "Stop fidgeting, Kenz, or I'm going to stick you with a pin. And I will not be happy if you bleed on the silk."

"You heard her, little sister. No blood on the silk." Lindy laughs. "That was handmade by dozens of nuns in some far-off land."

The glare I throw at my sarcastic sister-in-law through

three freaking mirrors is vicious. "I'm glad you're all enjoying my discomfort." Caitlin pinches me, and I kick her with the beautiful silver heels they had me slip on with the dress. "Ouch. What the hell, Cait?"

"Stop. Fucking. Fidgeting. Mackenzie," she growls around the pin being held between her teeth.

"I'm glad Nixon was there, and I'm glad he's taking you this weekend," Everly admits as she studies the lines of the dress on my body. "He'll scare this Dr. Dick off, and maybe him being your date will get a hot doc to look your way. You know how men are."

My beautiful blonde bombshell best friend never needed help getting a guy to notice her a single day in her entire life. And okay, so maybe I'm a little jealous.

"No, Everly. Apparently, I don't know how men are, since I rarely have their attention to begin with. How about you enlighten me?" And maybe my words are a little harsher than I intended. But seriously . . . if I knew how men were . . . *are* . . . ugh.

If I understood men, I wouldn't need a fake date, now, would I?

Cait places the last pin, then stands and adjusts her edgy black leather skirt. "Men always want what someone else has, or what they're told they can't have. And you're going to be walking in on the arm of one of the hottest men in the city. A star hockey player *and* a *Sinclair*. People will take notice."

She moves across the room to put away her pins, and Everly and Lindy nod in agreement.

"I don't have time for a man, ladies. I work around the clock, and when I'm not working, I don't want to spend my time fretting over a man." I turn so I can get a better view of the low, drapey back of the dress and the way the beautiful silk slides over my ass. "Caitlin . . ." I look over at my cousin. "This really is beautiful."

Long dark hair frames her pale, delicate face, and a smile spreads along her cherry-red lips, making her look even more like Snow White than her mom does. "I know."

"Four-inch heels, Kenz." Lindy moves next to me and lifts my hair off my shoulders. "And try not to kill yourself in them, okay?"

"Ha. Ha. Ha. I'm not that bad," I counter and step off the dais very carefully. No need to wobble and prove them right. "I was an athlete, remember?"

Everly unzips the hidden zipper as she ushers me into the dressing room. "We were all athletes, Kenz."

"I seem to remember being the captain of the team and beating your tiny ass for the spot on the all-state team," I correct her.

"Come on, Kenz. You've got to admit if you're not in sneakers or soccer cleats, you've always been a bit of a klutz." She holds her hand out for the dress and waits as I slip out of the silk and back into my jeans and sweater.

She's not wrong, but I refuse to acknowledge that out loud. "So . . . you're not mad about me taking Nixon to the event?" I pull on my riding boots and throw my hair up into a bun. "Because I can bail on the whole thing if it's a big deal."

I wait, practically hoping she'll tell me she's uncomfortable and that she'd rather I not go with her brother.

It would be a fantastic excuse.

But I have great friends who would never do that to me.

Damn it.

Everly opens the door and waits for me to walk through it before following behind. "Nope. Not a biggie at all. I hope Nixon scares the piss out of Dr. Dick. And Cross and Ares and Easton will all be there if Nixon needs backup. They'll make sure he knows to keep his hands, his leers, and his creepiness in check and to himself. Look at it this way, your brother and three honorary brothers will all be there for you."

My heart sinks a little bit because somehow even my fake date just managed to get even more friend-zoned, if that's possible.

What is it about me that everyone finds so utterly unattractive that there isn't a man in my life who looks at me as more than a little sister?

Then I remind myself that I'm a twenty-seven-year-old successful doctor.

My mother didn't need a man, and neither do I.

It might be time to do some one-click shopping for a stronger vibrator though.

The Philly Press

FRIENDLY REMINDER

Why do we insist emotionally unavailable men are always hotter? Is it the chase that makes them attractive? The idea that we can fix them? This reporter isn't sure, but I was recently reminded, yet again, why it's so much more fun to write about sexy athletes than it is to date them in real life.

#KroydonKronicles #FriendlyReminder #PSA

Nixon

Chapter 4

"*D*ude. You should have seen her," Leo chuckles as he walks through our front door and carefully steps over Gordie Howe, my lazy bulldog, who's been waiting patiently for us to get home. "She was fucking perfect. Blonde hair, blue eyes . . ."

"*Dude,*" I mock him before he gets the chance to keep going, then bend down and scratch Gordie behind his ears as Leo walks into the kitchen. "You realize you just described our sisters and half our family, right?"

My phone rings as Leo drops his hockey bag against the wall and grabs something from the fridge. It's my agent, Hunter, *again.*

I send it to voice mail.

"Grace has had brown hair for years. So really, I'm just describing . . ." His words die off like he just realized I'm right. Took him long enough.

"Okay, yeah . . . What-the-fuck-ever. You made your point. But she was hot and stacked and looked nothing like our sisters. Don't ruin it for me because I choose not to live like a monk. What crawled up your ass anyway?"

"Who's living like a monk?" comes from a groggy voice in the living room.

Both our heads spin to the couch where Callen is lying, one arm thrown over his face, half asleep, but apparently awake enough to be listening to our conversation.

Gordie pops up from the floor and takes his good old time wandering over to Callen. My fat pup uses all the effort he can muster to push all his rolls up next to Callen before basically nut-punching him while he makes himself comfortable and crop dusts the whole room.

Guess he told him.

"Fuck, Gordie . . ." Callen sits up and jerks away from the smell. "You're dog's fucking gross, man."

"You're on his couch," I remind him and add my hockey bag to the pile. "What the hell are you doing here anyway? Shouldn't you be at practice, or I don't know . . . maybe at your own place?"

"Air conditioner is broken. They're sending someone up later today to fix it, but it's too damn hot in there. Especially after a brutal practice," he tells me like it's the most normal thing in the world to go sleep on someone else's couch. Guess I should be grateful he's not in my fucking bed. "So who's living like a monk? And I'm gonna need you to tell me exactly why either of you would willingly forgo sex. It's basically the greatest gift the world has to offer . . . Well, after football."

Callen chugs the family football Kool-Aid big time.

I'd call him one of the great football players of our generation. Well, not to his face. The fucker's ego is big enough already without the boost. Technically, he's my dad's generation, not mine. He's what we like to call an oopsie-baby. Something the whole family still teases him about as often as possible. Especially considering he may have been conceived on the kitchen table as my Uncle Murphy walked in, catching Grandpa and Grandma in the act.

Grandpa has coached the Philly Kings for close to three decades. Dad retired from the team a few years ago and is still known as the best quarterback the NFL has ever seen, and now he's the quarterback coach. Then there's Callen. He's been carving a name for himself for years. Another Sinclair at the top of the game.

And that's just the family associated with the Kings.

Can't forget the uncles who are retired Hall of Famers too.

What can I say . . . we're a family of overachievers.

Hockey vs. football is an everyday argument at family dinners.

Leo moves into the room and tosses me a bottle of water. "Yeah, Nix. Why the hell would you be living like a monk when you could have your pick of any woman in the city? I'm sure there's a few Callen hasn't already sampled."

Callen shrugs, and I throw the water at his head.

He catches it easily with one hand.

Fucker.

"I'm not a monk, asshole." I drop into the chair across from Callen and kick my feet up, irritated with my jackoff brother. "Just because I'm not as in your face about it as you two fucks doesn't mean I'm celibate. It means I don't need the world to know what I'm doing. I'd rather not have the *Kroydon* fucking *Kronicles* reporting on me once a month, thanks."

"Sounds like somebody needs to get laid, if you ask me. Could this have anything to do with the hot date you've got Saturday night?" Leo shoves Gordie off the couch and takes his spot. "Because Kenzie Hayes is smoking fucking hot, Nix. And she's a doctor."

"The hell?" Callen looks from Leo to me, like he couldn't possibly have heard him right. "You got a hot date with Kenzie you forgot to tell the class about, man?"

Oh yeah. He's pissed.

Now the question is—why?

"You got a thing for Mac you failed to mention, Callen?" I lean back in the chair and watch and wait. People can say whatever they want aloud. It's the nonverbal cues that'll tell you everything you really need to know though.

Callen's shoulders tighten, and his face pinches.

He might be pissed or possessive, but I don't think it's either.

He's being protective.

Interesting.

"You two are worse than the twins, you know that, right?" I clench my jaw, already over this shit. Definitely regretting mentioning it to Leo. "It's not a hot date. I'm helping a friend out. That's all."

Not sure I believe it, but maybe *they* will.

Callen drags his hand over his face in a move that makes him look so much like my dad you'd think Callen was his son instead of his little brother. "Helping out a friend, huh?" He sounds like he believes it as much as I do. "Whatever helps you sleep better at night, man."

Whatever I've got to tell myself . . . I kick that thought around in my head for a minute.

What the hell *am* I telling myself?

She needs a friend . . . I can be a friend. A friend who finds her incredibly sexy.

"Maybe you should try not sleeping alone. Might help with that . . . problem," Leo jokes, and if I had something to throw at him, I would.

"I don't have a problem," I grind out. "Other than the fact

that Callen never answered the question. Maybe he's the one who has a thing for the smokin' hot doc."

Oh yeah. I don't like the sound of that even a little fucking bit.

"I don't have a thing for Kenzie. I just don't want to see you get screwed because you're screwing around with some-body in the circle," Callen argues defensively.

"The circle? What fucking circle? Like the circle of trust?" Leo laughs and stretches his arms out like he's holding an oversized beach ball.

"Leo, man. You're not that damn dumb. Like our circle of friends. Like one of your sisters' friends. One of my friends. Your team's co-captain's little sister. She's in the circle. Kenzie being Kenzie makes things complicated. Trust me," he warns, and my guard goes up.

"You got personal experience with complicated, Uncle?" Leo pushes harder, and I've about had enough of this shit.

"It's not complicated, guys. I'm here to help. And if I need to step aside and let someone else do the helping, then let me know. If not, I'm taking Mac to the event this weekend and making sure Dr. Dick knows not to fuck with our *friend*. Now, if we're done talking about this, I've got shit to do." When no one adds anything else, I walk out of the living room into my bedroom, kick the door shut behind me, and face-plant on my bed.

The whole conversation left a sour taste in my mouth.

Not because I mind going with Mac.

More like the idea of someone else being interested makes me feel . . . something.

Angry.

Frustrated.

Possessive as hell.

All emotions I have no right to feel about this woman. But that doesn't change them.

Friends, I remind myself as I move the pillow over my head.

She's my friend.

My stunningly beautiful, incredibly sexy, intelligent friend.

Kenzie

Chapter 5

Netflix needs to stop asking if I'm still watching and start refusing to play the next episode until I move the wash to the dryer.

—Kenzie's Secret Thoughts

I toss a piece of popcorn in my mouth and tell Netflix, that yes, *in fact*, I do wish to continue watching the show I've been binging for hours and also confirming that, *yes*, I do not have a life. Why can't they just accept that I need a brain break, and *Stranger Things* always does the trick. Especially season one.

My phone pings with a notification that my Chinese food was just delivered to my doorman, so I force myself to pause the TV right before Steve and Nancy are about to have sex. *Poor Barb.* I throw on my comfy white beach sweater over my tank and slide my feet into my ancient Uggs. It might not be high fashion, but it's better than my boobs falling out and flashing our doorman, Chadwick. I'm pretty sure that man hasn't seen boobs in real life since the turn of the century.

My eyes are drawn to Nixon's door as I wait for the elevator.

Is he home?

Is he alone?

Does it matter?

I shake myself out of my thoughts on the ride down to the first floor and thank Chadwick for the food just as a roly-poly brown, white, and black furball comes bounding inside the building and slides across the marble floor to a bouncing halt on top of my feet before he starts sniffing my ankles. "Oh my . . . aren't you the cutest thing?"

I bend over and run my hand over the pup's big head, digging my fingers into his soft fur. I giggle as my new friend immediately rolls over and twitches one of his fat little paws while I hit an apparently good spot.

"Better watch out," the deep, sexy voice belonging to the man who has been haunting my thoughts tells me. "Gordie knows exactly how to play you to get what he wants."

"Is that right?" I ask, careful to smile at the dog. Not the man.

The man who looks deliciously sexy in a pair of gray sweatpants and a tight navy-blue Revolution t-shirt. His dark messy hair falls in his eyes, like he's run his hands through it a few too many times, and I wonder what it would feel like to dig my fingers into it.

He looks down at me with heat in his baby-blue eyes, and I swear for just a single second, his pupils dilate, and nervous butterflies take flight in my stomach.

Fun fact I learned in med school . . . It's clinically proven your body releases oxytocin and dopamine, giving your brain a boost, when you're sexually attracted to someone. Hence, your pupils appearing to dilate.

When I get nervous, I turn into a human encyclopedia.

And this is why I don't date.

Well, not the only reason.

Not even the top reason, really.

Lack of time . . . Lack of trust . . . Lack of decent men . . .

The list goes on.

We haven't even gone on our fake date yet, and I'm already a nervous wreck. How am I supposed to make any of this believable tomorrow?

Better question—*what the hell is wrong with me?*

This is Nixon. My best friends' brother who knew me when I had braces and bad glasses. It's never been weird between us, and now I'm making it weird.

And now I'm arguing with myself.

Way to go, me.

"Oh yeah?" I pull up my proverbial big-girl panties and try to look up at him playfully from behind my glasses. *Much chicer glasses now.* "He gets whatever he wants, huh? Did he learn that from his owner?"

Huh . . . I'm kind of proud of myself. That might actually pass for flirting. *Go me.*

A slow, sexy grin spreads over Nixon's scruffy, handsome face before he bends down to clip a leash onto Gordie's collar and runs his hand up and down the back of the adorable dog's neck.

The pup whines quietly when his owner stands back up, and I might actually be in agreement with the dog. I wouldn't mind this particular Sinclair running his hands along my body either. I bet he knows exactly what he's doing. Which would at least make one of us.

Oh. My. Goodness . . . And now I'm jealous of a dog.

"What'cha thinking that's got your cheeks blushing like that, Mac?"

His words are teasing and soft but remind me, yet again, how out of my league Nixon really is. I try to ignore him as I stand and head for the elevator, but the closer he is, the harder it seems to be.

"I'm thinking I'm hungry, and I ordered way too much food, judging by the weight of this bag," I admit sheepishly as we step on and watch the doors close us in. "I like to be able to have a little bit of everything, so there's always extra."

"It smells pretty damn good," he groans. "Way better than the grilled fish and rice sitting in my fridge, waiting to be warmed up."

"I've got plenty to share, if you're in the mood for some Chinese and Netflix."

"Mackenzie Hayes . . . are you asking me to Netflix and chill?"

A ridiculously loud, obnoxious laugh slips past my lips. "If *Stranger Things* and General Tso's sounds sexy to you, then I guess I am. But really think more Netflix and veg, less Netflix and chill. I need a night where I don't have to work or think or cook, or really even do laundry, since I haven't moved the wash to the dryer in about three episodes now."

The doors ding and open, and Nixon takes the greasy bag of food from my hands. "Sounds perfect."

Umm . . . Yeah. I guess it kind of does.

"*D*o you remember the way you used to stab the food with your chopstick?" I point my chopstick at him and laugh as Nixon drops his dumpling . . . *again.*

"Listen. I never understood why we needed chopsticks if we had perfectly good forks in the drawer." He gives in and picks up the dumpling with his fingers and pops it in his mouth. Can eating be sexy? Because the way Nixon does it, it somehow manages to be sexy.

"So what's it like coming home, Mac?" He swallows and leans back against the couch, since we're both sitting on the floor between my coffee table and the couch. I haven't exactly gotten around to buying furniture yet. It seems pointless when I think about how much time I actually spend at home.

I lean over his plate and steal a piece of the sweet and sour chicken, buying myself a minute to decide how I want to answer this.

"It's different, but I figured it would be. The girls have all moved on with their lives, and I feel like I'm standing still in some ways. So that's a little weird. Plus, I built a life in DC." I think about that for a minute and silently cringe. "Maybe not an exciting one. But it was mine. Don't get me wrong, I *am* happy to be home. I love being close enough to finally see everyone again . . . To actually be an active member of my family. It's just a little hard to . . ."

I trail off, trying to find the words.

"I get it. Leo and Hendrix stayed in town and went to Kroydon U together. They played hockey together. They lived together. Then I came home after graduating from Boston U and felt a little like an outsider instead of a big brother. And I got to see them a lot more over the four years I was away than you got to see anyone during your residency. It's like you have to try to reassimilate to this world." He grabs an egg roll and points it at me.

"Did you ever think about playing anywhere else?" I ask curiously. Easton spent years playing across the country before he was traded home. It's not like most players spend their entire careers in one city, playing for one team.

"I've thought about it," he shrugs, nonchalantly. "But I've got it good where I am. I don't know . . ." he muses. "But seriously, Mac. You've got to stop being so damn hard on your-self. You're not standing still. You're a freaking surgeon, which is amazing. You're delivering babies. That's so cool."

He takes a bite of his egg roll, then pushes away Gordie when he lifts his head, wanting to see what Nix is crunching on. "What made you decide to be an ob-gyn?"

I place my plate on the table and wipe my hands with a napkin, buying myself a minute or two. "You want the real answer or what I tell everyone?"

He doesn't hesitate. "The real answer."

I turn toward him and bring my knees up in front of myself. "The worst day of my life was inside a hospital. My mom was young and beautiful and full of life a week before she died. Then she got the flu and just kept getting sicker." I think back to those days before she got sick. I can still hear her laugh. It's harder to remember now, but if I calm my mind, I can still hear it. I can still remember the smell of the French toast with honey and cinnamon she made us that Sunday morning and the way she was coughing and calling it a summer cold.

Soon, all I could smell was the acidic hand sanitizer we had to use every time we went into her hospital room. My stomach drops like it always does when I think about that week. The way I was counting down the days until she could come home. The way Easton was so miserable, having to stay with our grandparents, and tried insisting we could just stay in Mom's room.

"One day, she was making breakfast and saying it was a summer cold. Within a week she was hospitalized. Within a few days of that, she was septic . . . and then she was just gone." Clinically, I know my heart doesn't actually hurt in my chest, but telling that to my head doesn't make a difference. I close my eyes and breathe in through my nose and out through my mouth, pushing back the pain. "Mom used to always tell me I was going to be a doctor. She used to notice, even at the beach, I hated my hands to be dirty. She knew then I was destined to be a doctor. Not just any doctor. She always said I'd be a surgeon. I guess I wanted to give her one last wish. But I want to be part of the miracle of life. So I got it in my head I wanted to deliver babies."

"Mac . . ." Nixon wraps an arm around my shoulders and squeezes, and I open my eyes to look at him. His face is a mask of emotion. "I can't imagine how hard that had to be."

I lean into him and rest my head on his shoulder. "Don't get me wrong. No doctor only gets to experience the good days. There are plenty of bad ones, and those bad days are horrific. You know you're going to be a memory in the worst day of someone's life. But I also get to be a memory in the best day of someone else's. Those are the days you enjoy."

Nixon's big hand runs up and down my arm. "You're pretty amazing, Mackenzie Hayes." Gordie takes advantage of the way I'm leaning against Nixon and jumps up, resting his paws between us and drags his tongue down my face until I'm laughing. "See? Even Gordie agrees."

"Yeah, well you're not too bad yourself, Nix." I allow myself another minute tucked against him like this, then scooch back and pick up my chopsticks, needing some space. I point at the dumpling left on his plate. "You gonna finish that?"

Nixon studies me, probably trying to figure out why I just jumped away like my ass was on fire. When he comes up without an answer, his easygoing smile slips back into place, and our melancholy conversation is long forgotten. "All yours, Mac."

I pick it up, and before I get a chance to eat it, he bites it right off my chopsticks.

"What the hell?" I giggle.

"Guess I decided I wanted it after all." His smile transforms his whole face, and then he winks and rises to his feet with Gordie snapping at his heels as he cleans up our mess.

I pick up our glasses and follow him into the kitchen, where he's already rinsing the plates and adding them to my dishwasher. He takes the glasses out of my hands and adds them to the top rack, then turns to look at me. His eyes soften for a second, then he rights the neck of my sweater that's slipped off my left shoulder and runs his hand up my neck, like it's the most natural thing in the world.

Only it's not natural for me.

It tickles, and I bite down on my lip and giggle as I take a step back.

"Ahh . . . ticklish. Noted. You better get some sleep. Big night tomorrow."

I cross my arms over my chest, very aware of his eyes on me. "You really don't have to go, Nix."

One corner of his mouth tips up, amused. "Wouldn't miss it for the world, Mac."

He leans forward and presses his lips to my forehead, and I suck in a breath, unsure what to do. I don't have to worry though. In his next breath, Nixon picks up his chubby puppy and heads for my front door. "Night, Mac. Sweet dreams."

"Night, Nix," I whisper so softly, I doubt he even hears me.

"Lock up behind me," he adds as the door clicks shut, and I'm left frozen in place, wondering what the hell just happened.

The Philly Press

COCKTAIL HOUR

Kroydon Hills Hospital is pulling out all the stops tonight for their annual fundraiser, and you know how much all the beautiful people in this town love to show up for a good cause. We all know what that means, don't we? According to my calculations, if we take one-part stunning sirens donning gorgeous gowns, add a shot of delicious men in sexy suits, and shake just right, we're bound to create the tastiest cocktail.

Stay tuned for the results . . .

#KroydonKronicles

Nixon

Chapter 6

HENDRIX

Dude. I heard you've got a smoking hot date tonight with your team captain's little sister. Thought you were supposed to be the smart brother.

MADDOX

Well, we know you're not talking about Leo.

LEO

The fuck? I'm smart.

CALLEN

Sure you are, man.

NIXON

This shit again?

HENDRIX

Is it again if it's the first time I'm hearing about it?

LEO

And you thought you were smarter than me.

HENDRIX

I am smarter than you.

LEO

Fuck you all. I'm smart enough not to date Easton Hayes's little sister.

NIXON

We're not dating.

MADDOX

Are you picking her up and taking her out?

NIXON

. . .

MADDOX

That's a date, young grasshopper.

NIXON

We're the same fucking age, shitstain.

CALLEN

You've been warned.

HENDRIX

Do we need to slow this down for ya, Leo?

LEO

I'm going to knock your fucking teeth in when we play your team next month, little brother.

HENDRIX

You can try.

Hey Nix. Just remember to wrap that shit up. Twins run in our family.

CALLEN

Truth.

LEO

Ohh . . . could you imagine if he knocked up Easton's little sister with twins?

MADDOX

Well, you know the Wilders are knocking up your sisters left and right. I wouldn't go throwing stones . . . Glass houses and all.

HENDRIX

Fucking sick, Madman. Why you gotta go there?

LEO

I'm with Henny on that one, man. Too far.

HENDRIX

Don't call me Henny, fuckface.

NIXON

I'm not knocking anybody up, assholes. I gotta go. Talk soon.

KILLIAN

Dude . . . wait. I'm catching up. Nix – you're dating Kenzie?

HENDRIX

Guess I'm not the last to know.

LEO

You gonna call Killer stupid too, Henny?

HENDRIX

Nope. I'm smart enough not to call an MMA champ stupid.

KILLIAN

You're both stupid. I don't need to kick anyone's ass. Jules will kick it for me.

MADDOX

Truth.

CALLEN

Make smart choices, kids.

> NIXON
>
> Yes, dad.

> CALLEN
>
> Ohhh . . . I like it when you call me daddy.

> NIXON
>
> And. I'm. Out.

I slide my jacket on and grab my wallet, a little less sure of tonight than I was before those stupid text messages. Not because I'm worried about what Easton will think. I've heard the stories from back in the day before he wifed up Lindy. He was way fucking worse than I've ever been with the puck bunnies.

What the hell can he say to me?

You're not good enough for my sister because you've done the same shit I have?

This girl. This girl was legitimately my first wet dream. She was the fantasy. Now she's the girl you bring home to mom. The only problem with that is I don't want to bring anyone home to Mom. Not yet. Hockey isn't like football. I'm not going to be playing into my forties like my dad did. The wear and tear on your body is different on the ice. I've got maybe another five to seven years where I can play at this level, and I don't want to split that focus between a family and the team. Not even for Mac.

"You look good, brother." Leo looks me over as I walk into the living room. *Madden* is on the TV, and his team is currently killing the Kings. Guess he's got his own daddy issues. Gordie's sleeping by his side. My dog isn't what's considered a sporty dog. His happy activity level is moving between nap spots. But my whole family has grown up with bulldogs. They're loyal little assholes.

"Thanks, man." I straighten my jacket and pocket my cell-phone. I don't know a thing about style and give even less of a shit about it, if that's possible. Caitlin's been basically styling me for a few years now. Even before she started working for Everly. We were roommates when I was a rookie, and she informed me I looked like a color-blind college kid instead of a professional athlete. She took my credit card, went shopping, and informed me she was my stylist. "At least Caitlin didn't make me wear a tie."

"Gotta give it to her . . . she's good. Have fun tonight. But not too much fun. I don't feel like having to tell Mom and Dad that Easton Hayes killed you."

"Always got to be a shithead, don't you, Leo?"

"Yup." He looks back over to his game. "Just don't fuck anything up, Nix."

Don't fuck it up.

Shouldn't be too hard.

I'm proved wrong a minute later. Mac opens her front door, and damn . . . she's . . .

Damn . . . She's beautiful.

Her dark hair hangs down around her bare shoulders in long waves, covering the thin pink silk straps of her dress. Her dress hugs her perfect chest and tiny little waist before it flares out around her legs.

She's my sisters' best friend.

My team captain's little sister.

She's in the damn circle, like Callen said.

I'm here to keep the dickhead doctor away from her and maybe make her smile.

She's got a great fucking smile.

I open my mouth before Mackenzie puts a frazzled finger up in front of her beautiful face. "Give me one more minute."

She disappears down the hall as I step through the door and pull it shut behind me. The same moving boxes from the other night sit stacked taller than Mac in the corner of the room, untouched. An oversized chair, small couch, and coffee table seem to be the only pieces of furniture she has. Out here, anyway. Her television hangs above her fireplace, surrounded by a few candles in what appears to be the only area she spends any time. Judging by the lack of furniture and the way she refuses to unpack, I get the impression she may not be staying for long.

"Hey, sorry . . ." She walks back into the room, slightly out of breath and so fucking beautiful, I lose any thought I may have had. "I broke the heel on my shoe and had to find another." She lifts her foot up in a little kick. A silver heel with a little ankle strap winks back at me as her eyes crinkle. "Crap. Where's my wrap?"

She spins in a tornado of anxious energy as I pick up the pink silk from the back of the couch and grab her shoulders. "Slow down and take a breath, Mac." I wrap the pink silk around her delicate shoulders and bend my knees, bringing myself eye level with her. "You okay? You seem a little . . ."

"Neurotic?" she asks behind closed eyes.

"I was going to say nervous." Her eyes stay closed, and it makes my skin crawl. "Look at me, Mac."

Wide honey-brown eyes fly open, and her lips part on a little O.

Fuck me . . . I take a step back, needing the distance. "You good?"

Mackenzie nods. "Sorry. It's been a long day." She exhales, and her shoulders seem to shake before she smiles a pitiful excuse for a smile. "I broke one of the shoes Caitlin gave me, and my hair wouldn't do anything, and I poked myself in the eye with the mascara, and now it won't stop tearing." She leans her head against my shoulder. "I'm a mess."

"Don't worry, Hayes. No one is going to be looking at your shoes." I lift her face until I've got her eyes. "There won't be a soul there looking at your shoes, Mac. You look beautiful."

A pink flush spreads over her cheeks, then down her neck and over her chest.

It's the kind of flush that has a man thinking bad thoughts.

Thoughts he's not supposed to have about his *friend*.

I take a step back and offer her my hand. "You ready?"

"Will you think less of me if I say no?" she asks quietly.

"Not your scene?" *Way to ask the fucking obvious, Sinclair.*

"Not really. I kinda skipped the whole how to be social in your twenties thing and spent every extra minute I had studying. Now my version of a fun night is getting a burger from West End and binging season two of *Stranger Things*." Her hair tickles my nose as she turns away from me to grab her purse. Sugar and citrus fills my senses and makes my stomach growl. Does her skin taste like sugar? Does her—"Ohh . . . One of those BBQ bacon cheeseburgers with truffle fries. Doesn't that sound good?"

"Sounds delicious." I swallow and follow her to the elevator.

Fucking hell. It's going to be a long night.

Kenzie

*T*hunder claps over head as Nixon and I walk into the ballroom at the Kroydon Plaza Hotel. The perfect ominous soundtrack for what is destined to be a disaster of an evening, if my day so far is any indicator. I tense when the first person I see is Dr. Dick.

"Hey now," Nix whispers. "You want to get out of here?"

I push my shoulders back and shake my head. "I promised Wren I'd show up for the practice tonight. I just really don't know how long I'm going to last."

"How about . . ." Nix's full lips tip up on one side—lips I want to feel pressed against my skin.

Women pay good money to have the kind of full lips and long lashes this man has been blessed with, only in no way do they look the least bit feminine on him. *Nope*. Not. At. All.

Nixon Sinclair's picture should be in the encyclopedia next to the phrase *alpha male*.

Encyclopedia . . . ?

Who the fuck even uses an encyclopedia anymore?

"What do you think?" he asks me, and I realize I totally blocked out whatever he just said. My God. I need this day to be over. When I just look at him blankly, he laughs. "Come on. Have some fun with me tonight, Mac. Pick a code word. If it all gets to be too much, just say the word, and we're out of here. But at least try first, okay?"

Holy hell. Did this man have a whole conversation with me while I was busy wondering what his lips would feel like on mine? "Like a safe word?" I squeak.

"No," he chuckles, and the sound is deep and gravelly and way sexier than it should be. "Get your mind out of the gutter, Hayes. Like a *you say the word and we leave* word."

I shrug. "Sounds like a safe word to me."

Nixon's hand skims up my neck, and his callused thumb brushes along my jaw, sending delicious shivers dancing down my skin. "Baby, if you want to play with safe words, we can leave now."

My jaw all but hits the floor, and Nix takes a step back and drops his hand. "Yeah . . . let's stick to code words, Kenz."

Kenz. He never calls me that.

"Nixon," a beautiful woman I'd recognize anywhere glides over to us. Annabelle Sinclair was one of my favorite people in the world growing up. Maybe because something about her always reminded me of my mom in a way Jules never could. Not that Juliette didn't do everything in her power to take care and love Easton and me after our mom died, but it was different. Jules is our cousin. I grew up loving her and looking at her as a cousin . . . before she morphed into a surrogate mother. She was never my mom. After Mom's death, Jules tried to love me enough for her and my mom, but it was always going to be different.

Annabelle was my best friends' mom, and she was, and still is, just one of those moms you knew loved being a mother. She made it look easy, and if you were one of the lucky kids her kids loved, then she embraced you like you were hers.

I used to love being at the Sinclairs' house.

"Oh my goodness, Mackenzie . . ." she gasps and steps between Nixon and me, then takes my hands in hers and looks at me. "Look at you." She smiles warmly, and out of the corner of my eye, I catch Nixon talking to his father, who's also come over. "I heard the girls mention you were home. How are you, sweetheart?"

"I'm great, Belle. It's good to finally be home." I give her my go-to answer and watch her eyes narrow. She knows there's more, but she's kind enough not to call me out on it here.

"Well, we missed you, so we'll take it." Finally, she glances over at her oldest son before looking back at me. "And why didn't I know that you were both coming to tonight's event?"

Nixon leans in and kisses his mother's cheek. "Sorry, Mom. I meant to stop by the house earlier in the week, but time just got away from me."

Annabelle's eyes dance between the two of us. "It looks like there's quite a few things that you got away without telling me, Nixon."

"Leave the kid alone, Belle," her husband practically croons her way as he places a hand on his wife's hip. "He's coming over tomorrow for dinner after the Kings game."

"Am I?" Nix asks before he realizes what his father just did and shakes his head. "Well played, old man."

Annabelle beams, and Declan smirks. "I might be old, but I know exactly how to get my wife what she wants. See you tomorrow night, kid." Then Declan leans in and kisses my cheek. "You should come too, Mackenzie. I heard Jules and Becket are in DC for the week. Bet it's been a while since you've had a home-cooked meal."

"Takeout sweetheart." Annabelle pats Declan's chest. "Don't get their hopes up."

"Thank you for the offer, but I'm on call tomorrow," I tell them, unsure whether they know Nixon and I aren't *together*.

"Honey, you have to eat, and our house is closer to the hospital than the condos are." She links her arm through Declan's and smiles like the issue is settled. "It's a one o'clock game. Dinner will be at six, and I expect you there. Now, I see Max Kingston, and I think since he's got two of my sons on his team, I might be able to get a big donation from the Revolution. If you'll excuse us." She tugs Declan with her, and I watch as the two of them cross the room to Max.

"Your mom is a force of nature," I tell Nix in awe.

"She's something." He palms the small of my back and guides me to our table. "She also knows exactly how to get her way. Could you even imagine trying to wrangle five kids and my Uncle Tommy if she didn't?" He pulls out my chair and waits for me to sit before taking his own seat. "Hope you didn't have plans for tomorrow night because you know she's going to expect you there."

"We'll see. I really am on call." I take a sip of water and look around. "Dr. Dick at three o'clock."

Nixon leans his face into mine, and I can only assume it

looks as intimate as it feels when his breath skims my skin. "He's been watching you since we walked into the ballroom. I've gotta ask, Mac, if he bothers you this much, why don't you report him?"

I want to crawl out of my skin. Not just because I hate that he thinks I'm so weak I can't report Dr. Dick. But also because I don't want my pity date to know just how much he's affecting me with barely a touch. "It's not that easy, Nix. Trust me," I quietly answer and suck in a breath as his fingers run over my bare back.

"Nothing worth doing ever is," he murmurs, even closer if that's possible, and I feel that tiny touch *everywhere*. "Are you scared of him?"

My words die in my throat as his fingers trail down my spine. "Uncomfortable is different from scared," I admit on a shaky breath.

"Am I making you uncomfortable, Mackenzie?"

Why is his voice so damn sexy, and why am I finding it hard to speak?

Another head shake.

"Then why are you trembling?" he whispers, his warm breath skimming my ear.

And damn him for noticing.

"Mackenzie . . ." he murmurs, quietly demanding an answer.

"Because it's been . . ." I hesitate to finish my thought and luckily don't have to when Lindy and Easton take their seats at our table. *Loudly.*

"Hey lady." Lindy smiles, clearly seeing my discomfort and loving it.

I'm going to kill her.

Easton waits for Lindy to sit next to me before taking the seat on her other side and glaring at Nixon.

Oh no.

"I hear you're doing my sister a favor, Sinclair." My brother sounds like every overbearing asshole I've ever known, and I roll my eyes. "You two look awful close for just a favor."

I take it back. I *am* going to kill him.

But I can't off them both. I refuse to do that to my niece and nephew.

"You know he is, Easton." My words are short but fired back at him with heat. "Back off." I want to crawl in a hole and hide . . . As if this isn't humiliating enough.

"I wouldn't call taking a beautiful woman on a date a favor, Hayes." Nixon drapes his arm along the back of my chair, daring Easton to say something, and I bring my eyes to Lindy, silently pleading for her to get my brother under control.

Wait . . . did he just call me a beautiful woman?

"Just keep your hands to yourself, Sinclair."

"Or what, Hayes?" Nixon asks, no longer sounding friendly.

This is seriously not happening.

Lindy shakes her head at my overprotective turd of a brother, who looks about two seconds from launching himself at Nixon.

Okay. Time to stop this before it starts. I stand and hold out my hand to my pity date. "Dance with me."

Nixon's baby blues light up with something that looks a whole lot like victory.

Nix leans in, and his lips skim my ear. "Did you pick that safe word yet, Mac?"

Oh, damn . . . I think I'm in over my head.

Kenzie

Chapter 7

*N*ixon takes my hand in his and moves us onto the dance floor. A slow Van Morrison song replaces the more upbeat tune that just ended, and he pulls me in close to his chest. His hand covers mine over his heart, and if I didn't know better, I'd swear my own heart skips a beat in return. Only this isn't an arrhythmia as much as an overactive imagination.

One of the things I've come to realize I was lacking in DC was human touch.

It sounds silly with what I do for a living. You'd assume I touch people every day, so how could I be lacking it? But that kind of touch isn't intimate. It's just not the same. Not the way I've experienced it since coming home.

I missed *this*.

This . . . Dancing closely with a man. Hugging my friends. Holding my niece in my arms. It's jumping on Nixon's back and the way my brother kisses the top of my head. All the little things everyone else does so easily every day . . . everyone but me, and I'm only just beginning to remember what I was missing.

Or it could be me just overthinking. *Again*.

Nixon wraps an arm around my back, and his big palm presses gently between my shoulders. I stiffen at first, caught slightly off guard. "Sorry about him."

"What do you have to be sorry about? Your brother *should* be overprotective. It's our job as brothers. Be grateful you only have one. Everly and Grace have three."

"I guess," I agree, slightly mortified not only by my brother's actions but also by my spiraling thoughts as I lean into Nixon's warmth.

"Why do I make you nervous, Mac?"

I can't blame him for the question. I'm doing a lousy job of hiding it. "It's not you, Nix. I'm just not used to . . . *this*." I blow out a breath, trying to figure out how to explain it to him without sounding like a fool. "To guys like you."

"Guys like me?" He does that thing again where he bends his knees so we're eye to eye, and I really wish I knew why the hell I find that so incredibly sexy. "Should I be insulted?"

Luckily, he seems amused, not annoyed.

"No, Nix. I promise it's not an insult. Not at all. Guys like you," I stammer, trying to put my feelings into words. Words that will preferably not completely humiliate me. But I fear it's too late. "Flirty guys. *Touchy guys.* Cool, confident, cocky guys . . . I'm not used to it."

He holds my eyes with his for a long beat before straightening back to his full, impressive height without backing away.

If anything, he pulls me closer.

Holds me tighter.

"Wait a minute . . ." The grin he gives me should be illegal, it's so potent. "The guys in DC aren't touchy? Poor fucks don't know what they're missing. There's nothing like a woman's soft skin." His fingers trail up my neck, sending a chill down my spine, and Nixon's eyes crinkle before they narrow on me. "There were guys, right? Probably chasing after you the way they did in high school."

I look away instead of answering, debating how much I want to tell him and wondering what the hell he thought he saw in high school. Because my recollection and his seem very different.

"What?" he asks as his hand cups the back of my neck and lifts my face to his.

"No, Nix. They weren't chasing me. Not in high school and certainly not during my residency. We were all too busy for that. Quick hookups were all most of us had time for."

A muscle twitches in Nixon's jaw, and I add it to my growing list of all the things I find surprisingly sexy about the twins' brother. "I know we're friends, but I'm not sure I want to be the kind of friend who hears about your hookups, Mackenzie." His voice rumbles deep and gravelly, and *ho-ly wet panties*. That sound reverberates like it has a direct line to all eight thousand nerve endings in my clit.

All. Eight. Thousand.

"You're safe then," I admit as a hot flush creeps up my cheeks. "No hookups."

The song changes again. A more sultry beat plays, and it's like we're two magnets drawn to each other. Each inching the tiniest bit closer. Almost involuntarily.

Nixon's hold on my throat can't possibly not look possessive.

It certainly feels that way, and I don't hate it.

"Did you have a boyfriend my sisters didn't mention?" His tone is casual as he slides the hand resting on my hip over until it rests just below my waist but not quite on my ass.

Damn. I haven't had a man touch my ass in so long, I think I lost count of the years.

"No boyfriend," I lament. "Not since the tenth grade."

It only takes him a minute to realize exactly who I'm

talking about before he groans. "Come on, Mac. You haven't had a boyfriend since Allen Dyson? The fucking vacuum? *Seriously?*"

"Shut up, Nix." I push back against his chest with a laugh. This is the problem with small towns. Everyone is related to everyone, me included, and everyone knows everything. There's no hiding. "It was a few weeks before homecoming, and Everly was dating his older brother. In my defense, once I found out why they called him *the vacuum,* we broke up." My smile grows as I remember in vivid detail the hickey Becket found me trying to hide before he threatened to have Allen's entire family erased from existence.

Becks was always more dramatic than Juliette.

"Wait . . ." Nix draws out the words, and I know what he's putting together. This man was never a dumb jock. "No boyfriend and no hookups . . ." The tick in his jaw reappears. That jaw is chiseled out of the same granite his chest seems to be carved from. "Not since tenth grade?"

"There may have been a hookup or two in college . . ." I may also be stretching the definition of hooking up.

Am I actually going to have this conversation on the dance floor of one of Kroydon Hills biggest events of the whole damn year?

I drag my hand down his chest . . . his incredibly hard, beautifully muscled chest, and an idea begins to take shape. Probably a very, *very,* bad idea. One I'm not ready to give voice to just yet. *No* . . . Instead, I decide on a different approach. "Listen, we can't all have beautiful women warming our bed whenever we want."

"Do you want a beautiful woman warming your bed, Mackenzie? Because I've got to tell you, I'd give my left testicle to see that."

I shake my head slowly, enjoying the way his eyes darken as he licks his lips like he's the big bad wolf, and he's *hungry.*

"The left one?" I tease slowly.

That cocky grin reappears. "Hangs lower than the right."

"Makes sense then. Sadly though, you're not going to find me in bed with any woman. Beautiful or otherwise. Vagina is my day job. Not my night one."

The song ends, and the DJ announces the first course is being served as Annabelle takes the stage and the mic. The hunger lingering in Nixon's eyes isn't going anywhere, but instead of saying a word, he offers me his arm and walks me back to the table.

Guess I was saved from diving into that discussion.

But maybe jumping headfirst wouldn't have been so bad for a change.

Nixon

My brain can't stop working through all the different possibilities.

Can't, not *won't*.

Because there is no possible world where the gorgeous woman at my side, who has charmed everyone she's spoken to tonight, hasn't had a hookup since college. I mean, she's spent four years in her residency and another . . . what, three maybe, in med school?

Then in a whirling flash of chaos, I try to wrap my brain around the possibility that Mackenzie Hayes has a different definition of hookup than the rest of the world. Because there's no fucking way this goddess hasn't had sex in almost ten years. Is there?

Fuck . . .

After dinner, I stand at the bar with a Jack and Coke in

my hand, watching her dance with her brother, when my father stops next to me.

"Maccallan, neat," he tells the bartender, then follows my line of sight and smiles. "Your sisters told me this was just one friend going with another friend. But I've been watching you, Nixon. And you're not looking at Kenzie the way you look at a friend."

I lean back against the bar and sip my drink. "We can't all be you and Mom."

"None of you should be your mother and me. Be yourselves. Find your own way, kid. It's all we've ever wanted for any of you."

"Yeah, I know. I just don't think my way includes anyone else. Not right now." Mac catches my attention when she lights up, laughing at something Easton said from across the room. Fucking beautiful. "Hockey takes everything I've got."

"Don't give it so much that you've got nothing when it all ends, Nix. Because, and take it from me, it all ends. If it weren't for your mother, I'm not sure who the hell I would have been without football."

"You retired as the most successful quarterback of all time. The whole world knows who you are," I goad him.

"Nah. The whole world knew who I was on a football field. Your mom and you kids know *me*. Our family is the reason I never lost who I was. Hell . . . who I am. Don't pass up a chance at that, Nixon." He looks back over at Kenzie and Easton. "And don't fuck her around. Kenzie's a good girl who your sisters and mother love. *Understand?*"

I put down my drink, no longer thirsty. "I wasn't planning on it. But thanks for the vote of confidence."

"Always were more like your mother than me . . ." he murmurs as I head back to the table, waiting for Mac and Easton as they walk off the dance floor. "You ready to head home?"

Easton looks between us and shakes his head. "Touch her and die, Sinclair."

"I'm shaking, Hayes. *Seriously*. Terrified." I drop my hand to Mac's back and enjoy her sweet giggles. And man, does that sound do something to me.

Something her brother doesn't need to know.

"Yes. I'm ready to go," Mackenzie inserts herself, ignoring the testosterone flying between Easton and me. We're both joking . . . *to an extent*, but I have no fucking doubt he'd eviscerate me for her if he felt like he had to. I'd do the same for the twins. "Tell Lindy I'll see her later, E."

He drops a kiss on the top of her head. "You should stop by this week. Let's try to do dinner before the season starts."

"I'll figure it out with Lindy." She smiles, clearly dismissing him and grabs her purse.

No sooner does Easton walk away than I see Dr. Dick zeroing in on us. "Dick at six o'clock," I whisper in her ear, and peals of laughter slip past Mac's lips.

"Come with me." I press her forward and guide us through the glass doors out onto the covered terrace and into the shadows. The storm has set in, and the warm rain is coming down in fat drops.

"Do you think he'll follow us," she asks as she glances around my body crowding her into the shadows.

"What's his deal, Mac? Is he hitting on you?" I run a finger through her hair and push the soft locks over her freckled shoulder. "Does he want to be one of those hookups you don't have time for?"

"Don't make fun of me, Nixon Sinclair." Her eyes hold mine as she refuses to back down. "You don't understand what it's like to be so focused on one thing that you just don't make time for any others."

The air between us crackles while rain pounds down around us, forcing us together under the small overhang.

"I might just understand more than you realize, Mac. But not making time for something like a relationship doesn't mean I can't make time for other things." I drag my fingers over her soft skin and stop at her hip. "Tell me something, Mac. How long has it been since your last *hookup?*"

She licks her lips and looks away. Something I'm noticing this woman does often. "Can't we just say that it's been too long and be done with it?"

"Look at me, Mackenzie."

Her doe eyes snap right back up to mine.

"So it's been years since a man touched your skin?" I tower over her and plant a hand against the wall, forcing her attention my way . . . *and damn,* it's almost too easy to get lost in this woman. In her intoxicating scent. In the way she shivers and moves closer while I drag my nose up the length of her neck. *Fucking delicious.* "Tasted you?"

Her teeth press down into her pillowy bottom lip as she clutches my shirt in her fists. "I don't have time for a relationship, Nixon."

"Good, because I'm not asking for a relationship." I bunch the silk fabric of her dress in my hand but don't move a fucking inch. "I'm not looking to do the dating thing."

"Then what are you wanting to do, Nix?" she breathes out as barely an inch separates our mouths.

"I want to taste your come on my tongue."

Her pink lips form the sweetest O.

"I want to hear you scream my name as you're coming on my cock." I'm practically shaking with the need to fuck Mackenzie Hayes in a way I've never needed anything before. "I want to remind you just how incredible sex can be."

Kenzie's eyes widen as she purses her lips.

"Tell me you want that too, Mac. Tell me you're good without labels or expectations. Tell me you want what I'm proposing."

She traces the lines of my face with the tips of her fingers. "Not a relationship."

I suck her finger between my lips, and a pretty hum builds behind hers.

"Not a relationship. Just two friends, who are already *fake dating*, helping each other out. And when one of us stops needing or wanting *help*, we stop. Still friends."

"Friends who've seen each other naked," she says softly, but goddamn, those words pack a powerful punch.

I lean her back against the brick building, fucking desperate for her, and slide my hand up the warm, soft skin of her creamy thigh.

Mac's head drops back against the brick as she sucks in a breath.

I run a finger over the damp lace of her panties, and she rewards me with the sexiest sound I've ever heard. "Friends who share orgasms, Mac. And I want your first one now."

Kenzie

Chapter 8

*M*y body trembles with anticipation and for once, I try not to overthink.

Hell, I don't want to think at all.

Not this time.

I close my eyes and just feel . . . *Everything.* Nixon's body against mine. His rough hand moving over my hot skin. Skin I shaved and buffed and moisturized to within an inch of my life earlier. *Oh, God.* His big, blunt finger runs over my lace panties through my sex as my breath catches in my throat, while he . . . *Ohhhh* . . .

"Don't tense up on me now, beautiful," he coaxes as he buries his face in my hair. "So fucking wet for me already, Mackenzie."

He teases me gently at first while I cling to him, strung tight enough to snap at any moment. "Nixon," I breathe out. "We could get caught."

"No one will catch us, Mac. I will never let anyone see you like this." His voice is tempting and possessive, and panty-meltingly sexy. "I've got you, Mac."

He presses his lips at the hollow of my throat and drags his hot mouth up my neck.

Goosebumps cover my overheated skin.

My breath catches in my throat, and my entire body tightens beneath his touch.

"Why are you holding back on me, Mac?" Good lord, that voice. This man. He's barely touched me. Lace still separates our skin, and yet he can already read me like a book. He tugs on my lace panties, and the friction is unbelievable. "I'm not giving you what you need until you give me what I want, beautiful."

"What do you want?" I sigh, trying to sound in control, but so far removed from it, it scares me. I shift my hips to get closer to what I think I need.

He pulls his hand back, and the tips of his fingers skim along my lips, painting them with my own excitement, and I swear I practically come when his baby-blue eyes darken to the deepest navy, need staring back at me like a demon possessed. "I want to make you come."

Nixon grabs my face with both hands and runs his thumb along my jaw. He stares at my lips like he's going to kiss me, but changes his mind at the last second. "But I'm not going to give you that until you let go, Mac."

When he pulls back, I can barely breathe, clueless as to what to do next.

Nix drags his thumb along my bottom lip and groans. "What are you thinking, Mackenzie? I can see it all over your face right now. Tell me why you're holding back?"

I close my eyes, not wanting to talk about this, but knowing if I'm going to trust this man with my body, I have to be honest with him. How is it a second ago, he was teasing me through my panties, and now I'm about to discuss something I know is going to be humiliating?

One hand cups my throat, and the shiver it sends down my spine is nearly violent, it's so powerful.

"Because I don't know what I'm doing, Nixon."

"What do you mean?" he asks, obviously confused, and the tiny flicker of my humiliation grows.

"You don't get it, Nix. My analytical brain doesn't even know how to have this conversation." At least not without completely humiliating myself.

"You're going to have to try for me here, Mac. Because this only works if we're honest with each other."

Damn it.

I know he's right, but that feels like the only thing I know at the moment.

I push back against Nix's chest, hoping space will give me back a little of my common sense, but instead, my fight or flight instinct kicks in, and I ball my hands into tight fists until my nails score half-moons into my skin, reminding me that I'm here. *I'm safe.* And I'm in control.

I'm a grown woman, *a goddamned doctor*, and this is me taking charge of one of the few pieces of my life that I've ignored for years.

I know what I want, and it's time I fight for it.

I want to learn what I've been missing out on.

A huge boom of thunder crashes overhead, and I wait for the lightning that never comes. I could make him leave if there was lightning. We wouldn't be safe. And one of the few things I'm certain about when it comes to Nixon is that I'm safe with him. Maybe that's what I need to remind myself. If I want to explore this, Nixon is safe, and he's not looking for more than I can give.

I carefully roll the words around in my head while Nixon waits patiently before finally opening my mouth and just going for it. "I know how to get myself off, and while it usually takes me a while, I can get myself there . . ." I swallow down my mortification. There's no turning back now. "But no one else has ever gotten me there."

"Selfish fuckers," he curses, and I stop him before he says more.

"I've had sex two times—with one person, Nixon. And I'm pretty sure neither of us knew what we were doing. It was my freshman year in college, and it was awful. Both times, I counted the minutes until it was over, and luckily, neither time took very long." I think back to the guy. He was in my Chem class and about as different from Nix as he could be. Tall and lanky, quiet, and if I'm being honest, looking back, he was pretty uptight. In fairness to him, I doubt he had a clue what he was doing, and he definitely could have used GPS to help him find my clit. "After that, I guess I just didn't bother trying again. I had to work twice as hard as the girls and take twice as many classes to stay on top of my degree, so I threw myself into that and let guys fall off my radar."

"One man . . . two times, almost a decade ago?" he asks me cautiously.

"I just don't think I'm the most sexual person you'll ever meet, Nix. But I'd like to try, and I think I'd like it very much if you could teach me what to do. It's hard to even want to explore this with someone when you don't know what you're doing."

"Let me get this straight . . ." His face changes. *Hardens*. And I prepare for the rejection I'm expecting, reminding me why I needed a fake date tonight in the first place.

Nixon holds my chin in his hand, and butterflies take flight in my stomach. This could go really well or dumpster fire bad. "No man has ever made you come, Mackenzie?"

Oh wow. There goes that growly, possessive tone again.

Only we've agreed to no possession.

And that's a deal-breaker, *as sexy as I find it*, at least for me.

I shake my head.

"And you want me to teach you what to do in bed for another man?"

"There's no other man, Nix." The possession in his voice, the molten hot look in his eyes, the way his body leans into mine . . . it all empowers me to take what I want. I wrap my hands around his shoulders and lift up on my toes, bringing our mouths inches apart. "I want you to show me how good sex can be. I want to learn everything there is to know from something other than a medical textbook. And I want you to be my teacher. And when we're done, I want to be able to sit across from you at birthday parties for your nieces and nephews, and I want it not to be weird. When we're done, we're done. And we each walk away, no hard feelings. You asked me what I want . . . Well, that's what I want. But only if that works for you."

Oh holy hell . . . I can't believe I got that all out without blacking out. And I'm pretty sure I actually sounded like I was in control. *Go me.*

"Fuck, Mac . . . that's asking a lot," he groans and takes my hand in his. "You want sex lessons."

"Oh my God." I cringe. "I want you to never call it that again."

Mischief sparkles in Nixon's eyes as he pulls me out from under the dry safety of the roof until we're both standing in the middle of what's probably the last warm summer storm of the season.

"What are you doing?" I squeal as a smile lights up his entire handsome face.

"Lesson one." He spins me out like one of his ballerina sisters until I'm laughing while the storm soaks us both to the bone, then he twirls me back to him. "Not everything in life has to be so damn serious or textbook, Mac. You've got to take some time to have some fun."

I giggle, and he shushes me, "Shhh . . . Do you hear that?"

"Hear what, you lunatic?" But I do hear it. The music from the gala drifts out on the wind. "You're crazy."

Nix shrugs. "Yeah. But there's something to be said for dancing in the rain . . ."

Kenzie

Chapter 9

Sometimes, I add a task that I've already completed to my to-do list, just so I can enjoy little dopamine boost that comes with crossing it off. Now that's my version of satisfaction. Not sure what that says about me . . .

—*Kenzie's Secret Thoughts*

NIXON

Hey, you want me to pick you up for dinner?

It's the first thing Nixon has said to me since last night when he deposited me at my front door. No kiss. No talk about lesson two. He waited until I walked through my door, then told me to lock myself in before he left. Then he just . . . left.

No discussion. No fanfare. *Hell*, no talk about anything at all. Just *lock up.*

I stare at the message on my phone from the bed in the on-call room.

After giving up on getting any decent amount of sleep last night, I decided to stop by and check on the practice's patients early this morning. Since then, I've had two go into active labor and another two come in who are still hours away from delivery. Everything is quiet at the moment, but admitting that is typically the kiss of death.

NIXON

You've gotta eat, Mac. Might as well make my mom happy while you're doing it.

My pager goes off, as if my thought of quiet was all it took to piss fate off, and I admittedly breathe a sigh of relief.

Everything doesn't always look better in the light of day. And last night . . . well, let's just say I'm thinking it might be better if last night stayed buried in the dark. I can't believe I admitted I've only had sex twice. How am I supposed to face him now? He didn't even want to kiss me last night.

KENZIE

Sorry. At the hospital. Already been a long day. Please tell Belles I appreciate the offer.

NIXON

Okay. Have fun.

I sit there, staring at my phone.
Was I expecting him to guilt me because I have to work?
Maybe I was.
When my mom was still alive, she used to say she was

single because no one would ever understand her schedule, and hers wasn't half as hectic as mine is.

*T*hree hours, one emergency c-section, and a healthy ten-pound baby boy later, I finally glance down at my phone again. This time, it's two other Sinclairs texting me.

EVERLY

Hey! Missed you at dinner tonight. Mom said you were coming but got caught at the hospital. How was last night? Nix said Dr. Dick left you alone.

GRACIE

Mom sent Nix home with a doggie bag for you. It's from Nonna's, and we all know no one can pass up Nonna's chicken parm. I think there's some salad and maybe a strawberry cupcake in there too.

EVERLY

Guess you're knee deep in someone's amniotic fluid right about now and that's why you're not answering. Ohhh . . . Or you're getting it on with a hot doc in a broom closet. That always looks like fun on TV.

GRACIE

I'd be scared something would fall on me.

EVERLY

Ehh . . . That's half the fun. Fingers crossed he looks like McSteamy. He was hotter.

GRACIE

You watch too much TV, Evie.

EVERLY

Listen, Grey's Anatomy is my comfort show.

GRACIE

People die in every episode.

EVERLY

I'm there for the hot docs, not the dead
bodies. Don't be picky, Gracie.

For identical twins, the girls couldn't be more different in most other ways if they tried. And I'm not gonna lie, chicken parm from Nonna's sounds absolutely delicious right about now. But it's ten o'clock at night. I can't knock on Nixon's door and ask him for food this late. *Can I?*

I wrestle with that thought as I drive home from the hospital, freshly showered because tonight was a messy one, and I'm dreaming of soft clothes and softer pillows.

I'll eat tomorrow.

However, once I make it home and change into my softest cream sleep shorts and the matching slouchy sweatshirt, which are basically my version of comfort clothing, my stomach is still growling for that chicken parm. I can practically taste the garlic on my tongue when I look at my phone and debate whether I should call Nixon or maybe just shoot off a text. Seriously . . . I stare at my phone long enough to want to kick my own ass for being silly and overthinking on a whole new level, even for me.

As Brynnie would tell me—Time to woman up, buttercup.

There's chicken parm at stake.

I can do this.

It wouldn't have been a big deal two nights ago.

Why should it be a big deal now?

I let myself out of my condo and pad down the hall to Nixon and Leo's place and knock on their door. *See?* Not a big deal. I've got this.

Leo swings the door open with a goofy grin on his face. "Kenzie Hayes . . . fancy meeting you here."

I roll my eyes and cross my arms over my chest as he drags his eyes down the length of me. "Don't be a perv, Leo."

I walk past him into the condo, already more comfortable than I was five minutes ago, because this . . . *this* I can deal with. Leo has always been a bit of a goof and maybe a touch of a perv—but in a funny way. "I heard you guys brought home a doggy bag I'm supposed to pick up."

A bedroom door opens, and Gordie comes barreling out, nearly knocking me on my ass before I have time to squat down and love on him. "Take it easy there, big guy." I scratch behind his ears, and the tubby puppy rolls over onto his back, letting me know he wants some belly scratching. "I got'cha."

"Hey, Mac. I thought you were at the hospital." Oh, wow. Gordie might not have managed to knock me on my ass, but his owner certainly just did. Tonight's sweats are black with the red, white, and blue Revolution logo going down the leg. His hair is wet, and his shirt is blessedly off.

And oh my . . . That's a lot of abs.

Gordie decides while I'm distracted is the perfect time to pop up and lick at my face, and this time, he actually does knock me down. "Hey, Nix."

Nixon

"*G*ordie, come," I give my ornery dog the order just like the trainer said to, only he couldn't give two shits about me. He's planted himself between Mac's legs and is licking her face. Can't say I blame him. I'd rather be there too.

Yeah . . . Best keep that thought to myself.

At least for now.

Instead, I offer her a hand up, then smack the back of Leo's head as he laughs like a dumb fuck. "You okay, Mac?"

She dusts off her perfect ass, encased in teeny, little shorts, barely a shade darker than her sun-kissed skin. And *oh yeah*, my mouth fucking waters, and my dick definitely thinks it's time to start those damn lessons now.

When she said she'd never enjoyed sex and admitted she'd only ever been with one man, I may have seen red last night. Even in college, I knew to take care of *her* first before I took care of myself. Whoever the *her* was. And I played hockey for the top team in the nation. Let's just say there were plenty of chances.

Getting *her* off was always half the fun.

I want to fucking kill whoever it was that didn't bother to take care of Mackenzie the way she deserved to be taken care of.

Lesson one may have been reminding her that not everything needs to be so damn serious and thought-out all the time, but lesson two will be where the real fun starts. And now that she's here, it's going to start tonight.

"You okay?" I ask as the sleeve of her top slides off her bare shoulder, giving me a tantalizing glimpse of creamy skin dotted with freckles the color of her hair.

She arches a perfectly shaped brow and smiles. "I heard a

rumor there's chicken parm from Nonna's with my name on it in your fridge. Maybe even a cupcake too. Any chance it's still there?"

"Damn. The girls told you . . . I thought I had lunch tomorrow," Leo chimes in.

"Like your sisters weren't going to tell me." She flashes him a dazzling smile and man, she's a fucking vision when she's comfortable in her skin. I knew right away last night when she tensed up that something was wrong, but I had no clue what it was. And I never want her to feel that way with me.

"Ignore him. He's full of shit. We leave tomorrow morning for a three-day away-game stretch. He doesn't even need lunch." I palm the small of her back and guide her into the kitchen where the bag Mom sent home with me sits in the fridge. "How was the hospital?" I run my hand through my wet hair and push it off my face, tracking the way her eyes widen as she stares at my chest. "My eyes are up here, Hayes."

Mac rolls her eyes. "I told you before, Sinclair. Steroids aren't good for you."

She pulls herself up to sit on my counter, bringing her almost to my height. I wonder how this confident woman in front of me can be the same woman who was so unsure of herself last night. "What are you doing with Gordie while you guys are gone?"

"My parents are gonna watch him for me." I pull her bag out of the fridge and drop it on her lap. "Why? You wanna watch the little terror for me?"

"Maybe." She shrugs and peeks in the bag. "Man, that smells good."

"A little late for chicken parm, isn't it?" I tease her, wishing I had more food to stuff in the damn bag. Mac looks like a stiff wind would blow her away.

"Listen, Sinclair, one of us worked all day, and I'm pretty sure it wasn't you. Don't judge me." She closes the bag back up and beams. "I'll be sure to stop by the studio and thank your mom later this week. This was incredibly thoughtful."

Her pink tongue peeks out and wets her lips. "So . . . you're leaving tomorrow for a few days. Are you excited for preseason to kick off? Or are you just ready for the season to kick in? Easton always used to complain he just wanted to get the season started. He hates preseason. He always has."

"The team's been gelling pretty good in practice. I want to see how we do in an actual game. We're rookie heavy this season, so tomorrow night is gonna be a good first test." I plant my hands on her thighs and love the way she shivers right away. "I've been thinking about the homework I want to give you to do while I'm gone." My cock throbs at the thought.

Mac looks around, probably checking for Leo, who I heard head into his bedroom earlier.

"Homework?" she squeaks, and it's sexy and kind of adorable.

Never thought those words would go hand in hand.

"Yeah, Mac. Homework. My first game is tomorrow at two. Half our team will play then. The rest of the team will play at six. I should be back in the hotel room by ten. Are you on call tomorrow night?" My need for this woman grows with just the fucking thoughts I'm having when she shakes her head. "Good. I want you to be naked in bed when I call you. Can you do that for me?"

"I feel like we've skipped a few lessons, Nixon." Her words are soft and sexy. Hesitant, but also intrigued. And I'm here for all of it.

"We haven't skipped any lessons, beautiful. I promise. I'll tutor you through every single one. You've just got to trust me. Do you trust me, Mac?"

"Yes," she tells me, and that one fucking word makes me feel like the king of the goddamn world.

Fuck . . . Does that make me Leonardo DiCaprio before the fucking ship sinks?

LET THE GAMES BEGIN

Hockey season is upon us, and preseason or not, I'm here for it. Bring me this season's newest hockey hotties, puck pack members, and all the drama that goes with these hockey gods. The town of Kroydon Hills bows down to you and all your beautifully delicious season-long shenanigans. Let the games begin and may they be ever in your favor.

XOXO – Kroydon Kronicles

#KroydonKronicles #PuckPack #HockeyHotties
#SeasonalShenanigans

Nixon

Chapter 10

The next morning comes too fucking early, and I'm filled with the kind of excited energy that only comes before the start of a new season. The first games are always the worst, preseason or not. I wasn't lying when I told Mac the team was gelling in practice, but until you're on the ice in an actual game, you just don't know what's going to happen.

When I was drafted to the Revolution, they'd just won the Stanley Cup and lost their coach. Coach Kane, my old college coach, came on board, and we all worked our asses off that following season to win our next Cup. But that was three years ago. We've made it through the first two rounds of playoffs these past three seasons, but we haven't been able to bring the Cup home again, and I want it so bad I can fucking feel it in my hands, like a phantom limb or some shit.

As soon as the captain turns off the seatbelt sign, I lean back and pull my hat down over my eyes. We've got an hour left. If I can tune out Leo next to me, it shouldn't be too bad.

"Move," is growled to my left.

Or maybe not.

I look over to see Easton staring down Leo, and my

brother is grinning like a little bitch. "Sucks to be you, brother," he snorts as he stands up. "Try not to kill him, Cap. We need him on the ice today." And as Leo moves into the aisle, the asshole laughs. "Plus, he seemed to make your sister happy when she was over last night." He salutes Easton and disappears down the aisle of the plane. Clearly with a death wish because I'm going to fucking kill him later.

Easton drops down into Leo seat and groans. "Does he have an on-off switch or something?"

"Has he ever?" I don't bother moving. Not yet.

"Guess you're right. You wanna tell me what the hell is going on with you and my sister, Sinclair?"

Jumping right in. I can respect that. Still not gonna tell him shit, but I can respect it.

"How long have you known me, man?" I wait. I didn't know Easton well when we were kids. He was a few years older than me, and he moved to Las Vegas once he was drafted a year after moving to Kroydon Hills. "I mean, if you want to just go by how long I've played for this team, it's four years. If you want to get technical, it's more like fifteen."

"She's my baby sister, Sinclair." His voice doesn't carry a warning. It's more like a plea. "My *inexperienced* baby sister."

When I raise a questioning brow, he shakes his head. "Don't ask. My wife talks about as much as your brother. Trust me when I say I don't want to know all the things she tells me. A man just doesn't need to know."

I sit up and fix my hat, more willing to show him a little respect, now that it's going both ways. "Then you should know she's a friend, and I'm helping her out."

Not a lie. It's all in the details.

He doesn't actually want to know more than that, whether he realizes it or not.

"Yeah . . . Just friends. That's how it starts."

"Friends, man. That's it. Nobody's getting hurt. No asses

need to be kicked. No threats need to be issued. I have sisters. I know what you're feeling," I try to satisfy his concern and ignore the piece of me that can't wait to call Mac later.

"You also have parents, Nixon. Kenzie and I have each other. And before you say it, yes, we have Becket and Juliette too. But it's not the same. Kenz and I have been through hell. Unless there was ever a time in your life where it was only you and your sisters, you don't get it. For days, it was just us in a house with grandparents we didn't know. Then we were thrown in Becks and Jules's house. It was still just us until it wasn't. That kind of trauma forges a bond you don't get. Be fucking grateful. But also be real fucking scared. Because my wife, my kids, and my sister are untouchable. And if you fuck her over. If you hurt a hair on her head . . . If you make her shed one tear—I'll destroy you. I don't give a shit that your sisters are my wife's best friends."

"Yeah, man . . . If I hurt Mac, my sisters would be the first ones to skin me alive. But I'm not going to hurt her. Like I said—friends," I tell him as I try to absorb everything he just told me.

He cracks his neck and closes his eyes. "Yeah. That's what I used to say about Lindy too. You're fucking screwed, Sinclair. Don't say I didn't warn ya."

"Consider me warned." I pull my hat back down over my eyes. "Any chance you want to sit there for the rest of the flight? Leo never shuts the hell up."

He reclines his seat and closes his eyes. "Wake me up when we land."

HUNTER

> You pay me to handle this shit, Sinclair. But I can't handle shit until I talk to you.

> Stop ignoring me or I'll fly out to your Leave it to Beaver-ville fucking Mayberry-esque town and knock on your damn door.

> Season starts in two weeks. Fucking answer me.

I'm standing in the box, waiting for the second game of the day to end with thirty seconds left on the clock when Easton slides next to me. Coach played him first period but pulled him from goal for the second and the third. No need to take chances with the best damn goalie in the league. Not when we're up by three.

We won the earlier game too, and most of us barely touched the ice.

Fucking exhibition games.

"You going out after the game?" Easton asks like he's not fishing for more than an answer.

"Nah, man. I'm going to bed. You?" I watch Leo deke Calgary's defensemen and shoot, but instead of the beautiful swishing sound of a clean goal, it's the clink against the bars of the net instead. Damn. That should have been a beautiful goal.

"Betting your brother's gonna want a drink after that shot," he pushes back.

I look away from the ice as the buzzer rings, signaling the end of the game. "Good thing there's twenty-two other players on this team then, isn't it?"

"You're calling Kenzie." He doesn't pose it as a question, and I think our goalie's gonna give me whiplash.

"What the hell, Hayes? You gonna pass notes in class for me too?" One minute, he's threatening me, and the next, he's asking if I'm calling her. "Are you trying to set us up now?"

"Fuck off, shithead. I'm just testing you." His voice holds a thread of teasing, and I can't decide if he's serious or not.

"Did I pass?" I ask as the guys skate off the ice.

"To be determined."

I don't bother to tell him I'm calling his sister or what I have planned when I make that call.

Kenzie

*T*he delicious, grease-fueled scent of West End cheeseburgers and truffle fries hits me as soon as I walk through my front door. *Again . . . ?* I drop my keys on my counter, grab a can of diet Coke from the fridge, and a roll of paper towels because I may be a surgeon, but I never remember to add paper plates or napkins to my grocery delivery order. I slip my shoes off before I walk into my living room and unsurprisingly find *Monday Night Football* on my TV. "You smell like Jose Cuervo and bad decisions. What are you doing on my couch, Callen?"

He pushes a to-go box my way with a lopsided grin. "First. It's Don Julio. Second. I wanted to watch the game, and the girls are watching some reality shit on our TV. I brought you a BBQ bacon cheeseburger as a peace offering though. Please don't make me go back. When Bellamy and Caitlin watch that shit, they scream at the TV."

"Like you don't scream at the TV during football games." I

take the spot next to him and moan when I open the burger box. My God, that smells good. "Where are Maddox and Killian?"

Once upon a time, the five of us girls lived in that condo.

But for the past few years, it's been a different five living there.

He offers me a shot of tequila, but I shake my head.

"I yell at football games. You're *supposed* to yell during football. They're watching ballroom dancing." He looks at me with scared eyes. "Dancing, Kenz. I can't get behind yelling at the TV during the cha-cha. I shouldn't even know what the freaking cha-cha is. Please don't make me leave."

I lean my head on his shoulder and relax.

I'm not sure how many nights we spent this way in college.

Too many to count, for sure.

"Who's winning?" I ask as I pop a salty truffle fry in my mouth.

Damn, that's good.

"New York," Callen growls back. He hates New York. The New York Nighthawks have been the Philly Kings' rivals since the dawn of time, according to almost every Philly Kings fan. Well, them and Dallas. "Just let me stay until half time. The dancing should be over by then."

I hold a fry up to Callen's mouth, and he bites it out of my fingers.

"I mean, you did bring me truffle fries."

*C*allen ends up staying until the end of the game, which is good and bad.

Good, because it's kept my mind off the phone call I've

spent my entire day hyper-focusing on. Bad, because when my phone rings at nine-forty-five, it's sitting on my coffee table, face up, when Nixon's name flashes across the screen.

Callen looks down at the phone, then laughs and snatches it when I try to grab it. "You two are going to be trouble." He swipes his finger across the screen. "Hey, man."

"Callen Sinclair—Give me that phone." I practically jump to snatch it out of his hand before he hands it to me and mouths the word *trouble.*

"Go." I motion toward the door and refuse to look at the screen until the door slams shut behind Callen. "Hey."

"I told you to be naked, Mackenzie," Nixon growls through the phone, and he sounds like a man holding on by a thread.

Something about that voice gives me a boost of confidence I didn't know I had.

"Did you want me to get naked on the couch with Callen, Nix?" I bite back with a little extra sass in my voice as I lock the front door behind Callen.

"Sounds like we need to set some ground rules here, Kenzie."

I don't like when this man calls me *Kenzie.*

Everyone in my life calls me Kenzie.

Everyone except Nixon. To him I've always been Mac. *Maybe Mackenzie.* But when he calls me Kenzie, I know he's not happy with me.

I turn off the lights in my living room and walk into my bedroom. "What kind of rules, Nixon? Because I'm pretty sure not getting naked with Callen is just a given. Not sure it needs to be a rule."

"Has Callen seen you naked? Because if you tell me he was the douchebag you slept with in college, I might just kill him, and that could make Thanksgiving a little awkward."

His lips tip up at the corners, but somewhere, hidden deep down, I think he might actually think that.

"No, Nix. Callen has never seen me naked," I reassure him as I get comfy on my favorite old Queen Anne chair and kick my feet up on the matching ottoman. It's one of the few things I have that was my mom's. Pale blue upholstery with beautiful white cherry blossoms and butterflies embroidered into the fabric. It's always been my favorite spot to do my homework, study for tests, and go over my charts for the next day. Sitting here is like getting a hug, and since it is my homework chair, I decide I'm feeling cheeky and going to use it for whatever tonight's homework is going to be.

"Rule number one—" Nixon's beautiful blue eyes deepen. "No one else sees you naked while we're doing this."

My back immediately goes up. "Amendment request."

"I thought you were a doctor, not a lawyer, Mac."

Okay. Well at least we're back to Mac.

"I was raised by a lawyer," I warn him. "If no one is seeing me naked, no one is seeing you naked either." I may not know much about what we're going to be doing, but I know my hard lines. And that's a biggie for me.

"The only people seeing me naked are the guys on the team. I can't do much about that."

"So can the guys on the team see *me* naked too?" I tease, not at all worried about anyone at all seeing me naked, except hopefully Nixon.

But that's yet to be seen.

"Fuck no, they can't, Mackenzie." There goes that possessive tone again, but this time I think I'm starting to understand it. And I'm definitely starting to like it.

"Okay, so no one sees either of us naked in a non-locker room situation. Got it." I snuggle deeper into my chair and wonder if I should have gone somewhere . . . sexier. The tub maybe? Should I light a candle? "Okay. I need some direction here, professor," I tease. More accurately, I guess I'm attempting to flirt. "Generally, when I get homework, I know what it is so I can study. I'm a notes kind of girl. Care to tell me what you want me to do?"

Why in the world am I this nervous?

Oh right. Because the hottest man I've ever known is on the other end of this FaceTime.

"I want you to talk to me, Mac." There is something about the way he says it. I can't place my finger on it, but it's sexy.

"What do you want to hear?" A hesitant waver is easy to hear in my voice, and the playful look on his face turns predatory.

"Tell me—did you like it when I touched your pussy?"

Damn. He went there.

I lick my lips and nod, but Nix isn't happy with that.

"Words, Mac. Tell me. How did it make you feel?"

I'm suddenly grateful for the dark room that gives me some semblance of cover.

"I felt . . . sexy." I remember the way my cool skin heated, just like it's doing now. "Hot. But with chills."

"Did you want more, beautiful?"

I almost nod again but stop myself. "Yes . . . I wanted to feel your hand under my thong."

"That's a good girl. Where did you want my hands? Did you want them on your legs? Your ass?"

"No," I whisper as my body heats.

"Did you want them on your cunt, Mackenzie?" He leans back on the bed, and I get a delicious peek at his bare chest.

Damnit, Nixon. Don't you ever wear a shirt?

"Answer me, Mac."

Oh hell. "Yes. I wanted you to touch my pussy, Nix. I wanted your fingers to circle my clit."

"Yeah . . . ? Is that how you get yourself off? Show me, Mac."

"What?" I gasp, not sure I can do that in front of him. "I . . ."

I bite down on my lip, forcing myself to stop that line of thought. "I'm dressed. I thought you wanted me naked."

"Changed my mind. The first time I see you naked, I need to be able to touch you. But I want you to do it for me tonight. Show me how you get yourself off. Pull the phone back and show me what you're wearing."

Oh damn.

Maybe I should have changed into something sexier.

I pull the phone back and show off my cute pink pinstripe lounge shorts and white v-neck tee.

Nixon's Adam's apple bobs in his throat as he swallows, and even that movement is sexy.

"Good girl. Now drag your hand down your body. I want you to feel your soft skin."

I close my eyes and do as I'm told, trying hard not to feel foolish.

"That's it. Now tell me . . . Do you use one finger or two when you play with yourself?"

"T-t-two." The word gets caught in my chest as I circle my clit. "I . . . I don't touch it at first. I circle it. I tease myself for a minute."

Now it's Nixon's breath catching in his throat. "Are you doing it, beautiful? Are you thinking about what it would feel like to have my hands on you, Mac? My hands are big. They're strong, and they're rough. Imagine one of my hands is cupping your ass while the other is working your pretty little swollen clit until you're begging me, and I can't wait another second to taste that sweet pussy." I gasp and open my eyes, locking them on Nixon. "That'a girl. You want to ride my face, don't you, Mac? You want to come for me? Tell me."

"I want . . . I want you to come too," I stammer out through short breaths, continuing to work myself.

"Don't worry about me. This is for you, Mac. Now show me. Fuck your fingers like you're going to fuck mine when I get home."

"Oh God," I whisper into the darkness, completely mortified as the tremors of my orgasm chase down my body. I bite down on my lip so hard, I'm surprised I don't taste blood as I come harder than I think I ever have.

"Fucking gorgeous, Mackenzie."

My already hot cheeks flush hotter, but not from embarrassment. More like empowerment.

"Next time, I want to get you off too," I tell him, high on my post-orgasm endorphins.

"Don't worry, baby. You will."

Baby . . . Did he just . . . ?

Nixon must catch his faux pas because his face hardens in the next second.

"You passed with flying colors, Kenzie."

"I was always good at solo projects, Professor Sinclair. It's the team assignments that are a little harder for me." I try to play into it, when I really want to call him out on his swift change of tone. "Guess I better practice. I'll see you when you get home later this week."

"Oh, there needs to be plenty of practicing. And good girls get rewarded for hard work."

"Well then, I guess it's a good thing I like straight A's. I'll be waiting for my reward."

And remembering this night whenever I'm in the mood to practice.

Kenzie

Chapter 11

Fourteen muscles are used when you pour a cup of coffee. Who needs to go to the gym when you've got a coffee addiction the size of mine?

—Kenzie's Secret Thoughts

*D*r. Wren Davenport is one of the top ob-gyn's on the East Coast. She's the owner of the practice I work for, and she's kinda sorta my aunt. Her full name is Dr. Wren Davenport-Kingston, and she's married to Becket's brother Sawyer. It's sort of the same with Becket and Juliette's son, Blaise. Technically he's my cousin, but Easton and I treat him like a little brother. One who's already taller than me.

The Kingston family is easily forty people deep these days, and we're worse than that old drinking game, Six Degrees of Kevin Bacon. Between us and Nixon and the twins' family, there's bound to be a connection to most people in Kroydon Hills.

When she and I spoke last winter, she mentioned she'd like to open up a second office in Kroydon Hills as a satellite office for the Philadelphia office. When she offered me the job, I jumped, like Simone Biles *high*. Not only was I being offered a dream job, but it was close to home. I mean, I could walk to work if I wanted to. I don't—because seriously . . . the heels. But if it wasn't for my shoe addiction.

I glance down at today's red patent-leather stilettos with the matching red soles. When your surrogate mom, slash cousin, is a former supermodel, she makes sure to keep you in nice shoes. It's our thing. I run my palms over my black dress and slide on my white coat like it's a superhero's cape, ready to take on the day when Wren knocks on my office door. "Good morning, Kenzie."

"Hey. I didn't think you were coming back until tomorrow."

"We wanted to be back before the weekend." She smiles warmly and adjusts my stethoscope. "How was the event?"

I narrow my eyes, already on to her. She's a Kingston. They're all nosey.

"Max ratted me out, didn't he?" Shockingly, he and his wife were the only family there.

Wren purses her lips but gives in to a laugh before long. "No. I actually heard it from a nurse this morning during rounds. When were you going to tell me you're dating Nixon Sinclair?"

"Maybe when *I am* dating Nixon Sinclair. We're friends, Wren. I just didn't feel like going alone, and his mom was one of the chairs of the event. Sorry to disappoint." I grab my empty mug from my desk and walk past her into the kitchen, well aware she's following me.

I pour myself my second cup of coffee this morning, then grab a paper cup and pour my coffee-addict aunt a cup as well and hold it out for her.

"When, huh?" She takes a sip and smiles deviously.

"What?" I ask, ready to go meet with my first patient.

"You said *when*, not *if*. There's a difference, brainiac," she teases and steps aside when I try to pass her. "You know you're done with your residency now. You don't have to work eighty-hour weeks anymore, Kenzie. You can have a life. In fact, I'd give it a try. It's fun."

I guess I did say when. But I meant *if*.

Totally meant *if*.

"Aren't you supposed to be in the Philly office today?" I snap, trying to change the topic. When she sips again instead of answering, I shake my head. "I've got a patient to see."

"You can run, but you can't hide, Kenzie. And if you think *I'm* bad, just wait until Juliette gets hold of you."

Well, that stops me in the middle of the bustling office. Without looking, I know all the color drains from my face. "You told Jules?"

She smiles. "Oh, honey . . . I called Sawyer, who I'm betting called Becket. And you know Becks wasn't keeping that to himself. Consider yourself lucky that you've been warned."

Lucky? . . . Screwed is more like it.

JULIETTE

We're flying back from DC tonight. Want to meet for coffee tomorrow?

KENZIE

Three whole hours, huh? Should I be proud?

JULIETTE

Maybe. But I'd settle for being grateful this text is coming from me and not Becket.

KENZIE

Really? **Insert rolling eyes emoji**

JULIETTE

Coffee at Sweet Temptations tomorrow, Kenz. Does ten a.m. work, or do you need it to be earlier?

KENZIE

My first patient is at nine. I can do eight.

JULIETTE

See you at eight a.m. Love you.

KENZIE

Love you too, Jules. Kiss Blaise for me.

EASTON

Just got a message from Becks. They want to do dinner this weekend. I told him I'd check with you. Does Saturday or Sunday work better for you?

KENZIE

Funny. I just got a message from Jules. She didn't mention anything about dinner. She wants to do coffee tomorrow morning.

EASTON

What are they up to?

KENZIE

They're fishing for information that isn't there. Saturday works for me. Thanks.

EASTON

You sure there's no info?

> **KENZIE**
>
> Et tu, Brute?

EASTON

Say the word and I'll kick his ass, sis.

> **KENZIE**
>
> I'm ignoring you. Have a good game tonight.
> I'm on my way to your house. I'm having
> dinner with your wife.

EASTON

We're actually flying home in a few minutes.
It was an afternoon game.

> **KENZIE**
>
> Have a safe flight, E. Love you.

EASTON

Love you too.

*L*osing my mother early taught me many things, the most important of which is don't take a single day for granted. Followed closely by make sure the people you love know you love them. Easton, Blaise, Jules, Becks, and I tell each other that often. Some might think too often, but Juliette and Becket made sure we never had any doubt, and for that, I'll be forever grateful.

They made it look so easy back then.

The way they loved each other.

The way they loved us.

That's the thought I have rattling around my mind when I knock on Lindy's front door before letting myself in. My nephew, Griffin, runs to me on his long lanky legs. "Aunt Kenzie's here!"

I scoop up the four-year-old and act like I'm going to drop him. "You've got to stop growing so fast, Griff. You're getting too big. What are you, ten years old now?"

He shakes his shaggy brown hair back and forth. "I'm not ten, Aunt Kenzie. I'm four years old."

"Four . . . What? I could have sworn you were in fourth grade. Not that you were four years old." I tickle his sides as I carry him into the kitchen to find Lindy cutting chicken into tiny pieces while she wears my niece, Elizabeth, in one of those wraparound things that snuggles the tiny baby close to her. Little Miss Lizzy doesn't like to be put down.

"Mom . . . Aunt Kenzie's here," Griff calls out as if we aren't standing right across from her.

"I see, big boy. How about you get down and go wash up for dinner, please?" she asks him sweetly, and I hide my laugh.

"Hey, Lindy. Did you know that Griffin is only four years old, not in fourth grade?" I ask dramatically as I settle the little monkey on his feet.

"I'm a big boy. My class is all day this year," he tells me excitedly. "Did you know next year, I'm going to be in kindergarten, but Lizzy won't even be in preschool yet?" He hops up on the stool in front of the deep farmhouse sink in the kitchen while I move over to Lindy and press my lips to the top of Lizzy's head.

"You can take her if you want. This is the witching hour. She insists on being held. If not, the whole damn street can hear her screaming." I carefully take my tiny niece out of the soft carrier and watch the way her blue eyes pop open and widen when they try to focus on me.

"Hey, sweet girl," I croon to my mother's namesake. She's

the perfect little mix of Lindy and Easton, and I can't wait to watch her grow. "Need any help?"

Lindy pours us each a glass of wine and pushes one my way. "Nope. Dinner is ready, the wine is delicious, and your brother won't be back for hours. Now take a seat and fill me in on what's happening in your life. I feel like I talk to you even less now that you're home."

She buckles Griffin into his booster seat and looks lovingly at Lizzy. "Do you want me to take her back?"

"I've got her. You eat." I sit down next to Griffin and snuggle Lizzy a little tighter, breathing in her sweet baby scent. "Well, let's see. I talked to Wren today, who apparently heard I was dating Nixon."

Lindy's mouth pops open. "Did you tell her you're not?"

"I did, but not before she told Sawyer, who told Becket, who told freaking Juliette," I moan. "Seriously, the Kingston family phone chain is off the damn rails, Linds. I'm surprised you didn't get a text already."

She smiles sheepishly, and I swear if I wasn't holding Lizzy, I'd probably scream. "Tell me you're kidding."

"Wish I could. Mom texted me earlier, asking if it was true." She runs her hand over Griff's mop of hair.

"What did you tell her?" I screech softly. Didn't know that was possible, but apparently it is.

"That you went as friends, but you didn't look like friends on that dance floor." Her big, blue eyes grow wide with excitement. "So tell me the truth. Is there something maybe, *sort of* going on with you two? Because the way that man looked at you . . . it was hot."

"You're reaching," I tell her as I push a piece of chicken around on my plate.

"I'm not, Kenz. Trust me. I'm pretty sure he's always had a thing for you."

"What kind of thing, Mommy?" Griff asks, and Lindy and I both smile at her beautiful boy.

"The kind of thing that makes boys smile at girls, sweetheart. The way Daddy smiles at Mommy." Talk about always watching someone. My brother has only had eyes for Lindy since he was barely twenty years old. Some things are just written in the stars. But that's not what everyone gets.

"He doesn't have a thing for me . . . Why would you even say that?" I ask, even though I'm sure she's crazy. Right?

"Kenzie, do you really not see it? You're smart and kind and beautiful. And Nixon Sinclair has seen that for years. I'm telling you, he has. Ask him if you don't believe me." She sips her wine, then rests her elbows on the table. "You and your brother are so blind."

"What do you mean?" Lizzy fusses in my arms until I adjust her again, then try to act like I'm not dying to know what Lindy means.

"Just keep yourself open to everything, Kenz. Don't shut down before you even give yourself a chance."

"You're not making any sense," I murmur, trying to string together what the heck ever she's talking about. "I know Nixon Sinclair is attracted to me. He's shown me that. But there's a difference between being attracted to someone and actually being interested in someone."

"I agree. There's a difference. But let me ask you this . . . are you interested in Nixon?"

Well, that's the million-dollar question, isn't it?

"I'm attracted to him," I admit and leave off that I got myself off to the sound of his voice the other night, then to the memory of that every night since. And maybe this morning too.

What can I say?

Having a healthy sexual appetite was never my problem.

Finding someone worth the time was the issue.

Is Nixon worth the time?

I'm sure he is.

But that's not part of our arrangement.

Lindy runs the tip of her finger along the edge of her glass. "So you're just attracted to him? You couldn't see yourself dating him?"

"I didn't say that," I admit softly as Lizzy starts to squirm on my shoulder.

"No, you didn't." Lindy stands and stretches her arms. "Give me the baby. She needs to be changed. And you need to decide what exactly you're saying. Take it from a woman who waited too long to go after what she wanted. Don't waste time on what-ifs. Life is too short."

Lindy takes Lizzy into the other room to change her diaper, and Griffin looks at me with mac and cheese stuck to his lips. "I'm not going to be short like life, Aunt Kenzie. I'm going to be as tall like Daddy."

"Yeah, big guy." I drop a kiss on his head. "You're going to be big and tall and have a really big life."

He beams up at me like I just made his day. Meanwhile, his mommy just threw a glitter bomb into the middle of mine.

Do I want Nixon Sinclair?

Yes.

Do I want a life with Nixon?

I haven't thought about sharing my life with anyone in years . . .

And I'm not sure I'm ready to do that now.

But if I were, Nix sure is one hell of a guy to count out.

Kenzie

Chapter 12

*C*aitlin walks out of Sweet Temptations, looking as fierce as ever, just as I'm walking in the next morning. Sky-high black knee boots, a black leather pencil skirt, and a black cardigan that only has three buttons buttoned in the center. Her black hair is artfully tucked up in a messy bun, which I'm sure took her fifteen minutes to look as perfectly imperfect as it does, and chunky diamond studs dot her ears. She rocks her confidence like she's never had a doubt in the world, and even though she's my little cousin, I think I want to be her when I grow up.

"Little overqualified to be doing coffee runs, aren't you?" I hold the door for her as she balances a bakery box and a cup carrier with what I bet are Lindy's, Everly's, and her coffee orders.

Cait's crystalline blue eyes look me over from the top of my head to the tips of my purple Jimmy Choo's. "We take turns. What's your excuse? Because seriously, Kenz. Those shoes belong somewhere more fabulous than Main Street."

"I promised Juliette I'd meet her before I need to be in the office. Is she inside?" Jules's office is across the street, so she may have stopped in there first.

"She's inside talking to my mom. Good luck. They look like they're conspiring." She turns toward Everly's shop before I call out to her.

"Conspiring about *what*?" My heart races in my chest. The Kingstons conspiring is never a good thing.

Cait looks over her shoulder and winks at me. "Good luck, Kenzie."

"Luck with *what*?" I ask as she heads two shops down to Everly Wilder Designs, ignoring me.

Damn it. Good luck with what?

If I don't go in, I could walk into my office in three minutes. It's only around the corner, right off Main Street. What can Jules say if I tell her I bailed for an emergency? I look through the huge picture window to see if I can make a clean escape, but I can't. I'm totally busted. Jules and Amelia, Caitlin's mom, are both staring at me from the table in the corner of the shop.

Time to pull my big-girl panties up, I guess.

I push through the door and wave at the two of them, then make a pit stop at the counter for a cinnamon pumpkin cappuccino with a shot of espresso and extra whip, because *really*, can you ever have too much whip? Once the extra-caffeinated goodness—which I'm fairly certain I'll need to get through what's beginning to feel like a strange ambush—hits my system, I square my shoulders and brace for impact.

Okay, I'm not generally a drama queen, but whenever Jules and any of *the aunts* get together, it's like you're going to war with a coven of powerful witches, each with their own special brand of magic. It's always safer to approach them carefully. That thought makes me smile. "Hi, ladies."

"Kenzie . . ." Jules stands and squeezes me in a tight hug, like it's been months since she's seen me instead of a week. "I swear I miss you more now that I get to see you all the time than I did when you were in DC."

Probably because Juliette called every other day during my residency. She'd leave me five-minute-long voice memos if I didn't answer, and sometimes Becks, Blaise, and she would send me a quick video just so I could see their faces. And she'd always stop by my brownstone whenever Becks and she were in town for any senate business.

She's a special kind of woman, and I'm so unbelievably lucky to have her in my corner. But I'm still a little nervous right now.

"Hey, Jules. How was DC?" I sit down between Amelia and her and side-hug Cait's mom. Amelia's not nearly as touchy-feely as the rest of the family.

"It was good. But I'm glad to be home. More importantly, how was your weekend?"

Amelia snickers and rises from her seat. "Real smooth, Juliette."

Jules rolls her lips in, holding back a smile.

"Kenzie, don't leave without taking some scones for your office. I'll go box them up."

"Thank you," I tell her as she walks away, and I turn all my attention on Juliette. "Go ahead. You know you're dying to ask." I inhale my cappuccino as she watches with hopeful eyes.

"I really am." Excitement is coming off her in waves. My cousin is one of the most beautiful women in the world. A former supermodel who's as stunningly beautiful today as she was twenty years ago. And right now, she looks like she's a teenager trying to get her friend to spill the beans. "What is happening with you and Nixon Sinclair? Sawyer called Becket and said you two were together at the gala last week."

"Sawyer has a big mouth for someone who wasn't even there," I murmur under my breath.

"Be happy the *Kroydon Kronicles* didn't run with it. Then

you'd have the whole town talking. So . . . are you going out again?"

"It was one time, and it wasn't a real date. When am I supposed to find time to date, Jules? I'm building my career. If I'm not at the office, I'm at the hospital or at home studying charts." I break off a piece of her pumpkin muffin and pop it into my mouth, buying myself an extra minute or two.

The excitement she had a minute ago changes. "Are you still considering applying for the gynecologic oncology fellowship?"

"I'm thinking about it," I admit, still not sure I want to commit to a three-year fellowship at this point in my life.

"Kenzie . . . I worry about you, sweetheart." She reaches across the worn whitewashed table and covers my hand with hers. "I don't want to see you hide behind your career forever. Take it from someone who spent a decade doing exactly that."

"I'm not hiding, Jules." I temper my voice so she doesn't hear my frustration. Jules and I have had this conversation before, and it rarely ends well. "I love my job. I'm proud of it, and I'm damn good. Specializing doesn't mean I'm hiding—it means I'm helping."

"I need you to really hear this, Mackenzie. I don't care if you're dating Nixon. I don't care if you ever date anyone. What I care about is you and whether you're living a full life. Work is only supposed to be a piece of that. You've got to fill the rest of it up with other things."

"Jules . . ." I want to tell her she's being dramatic, but I would never disrespect her that way. "My life is full. I have my friends and family. I have a job I love. And if I decide to do this, I'd only apply for local fellowships. I wouldn't leave again. I promise."

She tucks her hair behind her ear. "I've got all three of

you kids home right now. You can't blame me for wanting to keep it that way for as long as possible. Blaise has less than two years left before he leaves for college, and he's already talking about wanting to go away to school. I don't want to let go of you again."

"Jules," I chuckle. "You never let go the last time."

"Fine. I didn't let go. But can you really blame me?" I know what she's saying without coming out and saying it, and no, I can't blame her. When you lose someone so quickly . . . someone as young and vibrant as my mom was . . . it changes your outlook on life.

"I'm not dating Nix." I decide changing the subject is my safest move. "He was going, and I was going, so we went together. *As friends.* That's it. There's no story."

She cocks her head and stares. "Yeah . . . I've heard that before. I may have said it to myself a time or two."

"Oh yeah?" I steal another bite of muffin before she pushes it to me. "How'd that work out for you? Are you still friends?"

"Yup. Best friends. I married him."

My pumpkin muffin gets caught in my suddenly dry throat.

"There's always time, Mackenzie. And you can have it all. A career. A husband. A family. Whatever you want, you can have. It might not be easy, but the best things never are."

I don't need promises of an easy life. I can navigate difficult. I thrive on hard. The harder the better. I can take that and make it my bitch.

But what scares me enough to turn and walk away, is the idea that it can all be ripped away in a single heartbeat. That . . . I don't think I could survive that. Not again.

The Philly Press

FRESH MEAT

Rumors are swirling that we may have our first sighting and it involves fresh meat.

One fan favorite Revolution-*ary and* a member of Kroydon Hills' very own royal family may just be the first casualty . . . I mean *coupling* of the season.

Do you wanna guess who?

Only time and this reporter will tell. Stay tuned!

#KroydonKronicles #Revolutionary #KroydonHill-sRoyalFamily #FreshMeat

Nixon

Chapter 13

I'm on my way to pick up Gordie from my parent's house when I turn off Main Street and catch Mac out of the corner of my eye, walking into her office. And wow. She looks incredible. Heels that make her legs look like they go on for days and a form-fitting dress that shows off every one of her delicate curves.

Shit.

Eyes on the damn road, Sinclair.

The other night on the goddamn phone was one of the hottest nights I can remember having in a long damn time, and I didn't even touch her. But I knew it would be. How could it not? It's Mackenzie.

My teenage fantasy.

Fuck . . . she's my adult fantasy too.

I hit the Bluetooth button and tell it to text Mac.

NIXON

A little late to be walking into work.

KENZIE

You stalking me, Sinclair?

NIXON

Small town. On my way to my parents' house to pick up Gordie.

KENZIE

Have fun. I just had coffee with Jules, and I'm having dinner with the family tomorrow night.

NIXON

Mom would have all five of us at her house for dinner every night if she thought she could.

KENZIE

Jules too.

NIXON

Are you on call this weekend?

KENZIE

Technically, I shouldn't be, but I told someone I'd cover them tonight.

NIXON

Woman. You work more than anyone I've ever known.

KENZIE

Observant.

NIXON

A man of many talents.

KENZIE

I'm not going to argue with that.

NIXON

I've got plenty you haven't seen yet.

KENZIE

I'll keep that in mind.

NIXON

Have a good day, Mac.

KENZIE

You too, Nix.

Something about texting with Mac has me smiling like I've just won a game instead of sparring with this beautiful woman.

I drive past my mom's ballet studio and see the lights on in there, so I'm not surprised when I get to their house and Dad's truck is the only one in the driveway. I knock on the door and announce myself before I go in. We've all heard the story of my uncle walking in on Grandpa and Grandma having sex on the table when he was in college, and I'm pretty sure it scarred each and every one of my cousins and me. Just because Mom's studio lights were on doesn't mean I don't have to be careful.

"I'm in my office, son," Dad calls back.

Mom and Dad bought this place before any of us were born, and they never moved again. It's crazy to think about all the memories this house holds, and so many of the good ones with Dad are in this office. I walk in and find him behind his desk and Gordie asleep in his bed, next to the old man's feet. Looks like he didn't miss me too much. "Don't you have a walk through or something today?"

Dad takes off his glasses and leans back in his desk chair as he stretches. "Not until this afternoon. Grandpa had something this morning, so he pushed our walkthrough back. How were your games?"

"Good." I drop down into the leather wingback chair

across from his desk and look to see if Gordie moves. He doesn't. One eye opens before he yawns and goes back to sleep, snoring like a trucker with a two-pack-a-day habit. "Team seems to be playing well. We've got a few more games next week, then the season starts the following week."

"How did Leo play? I haven't talked to either of you this week."

"You know how preseason is. We're working out a few kinks, but he's holding his own. How about you? The Kings gonna make it to the Super Bowl this year?"

Nostalgia washes across his face. "It'd be nice, but it's too soon to tell. Ask me again in December. That's when bowls are won or lost before they ever get played. You coming to the game this weekend?"

I press the toe of my sneaker to Gordie's paw, trying to get some excitement out of him.

It doesn't work.

Lazy fucker.

"I'm not sure yet. I've got to look at our schedule. We play Hendrix's team the first week in October. I'll make sure to tell Mom so she can add it to the calendar."

"It's already on there. She's beside herself. She's never had her kids playing against each other before." He crosses his arms over his chest in a move so familiar I might as well be a kid getting punished for fucking with the twins' dolls or something. "Not a pro game anyway."

"I was going to say we played each other in college." I look around the room at the pictures lining the walls. Our family history on display. Us kids. My Uncle Tommy. Mom and Dad. Aunts and uncles, cousins, grandparents. Memories. That's what Dad always said mattered most in the world.

His number was retired, but there's no jersey hanging.

No rings displayed.

One lone football sits on a shelf behind him. It's his last

game ball from his final pro game. Every other thing in this room represents the people he puts above all else. He always knew the game would end. He always made us his priority.

He's a hard act to follow and an impossible man to live up to. He always teased us for playing hockey instead of football. Never in a mean way, but football was his first love before he met Mom, so it's hard to imagine he wasn't a little disappointed when all three boys decided to play hockey.

What he never realized was that, even as kids, we knew his shoes would be impossible to fill. It was easier to find our own. And three would-be football princes decided they wanted to be hockey kings instead.

"I think your mother blocked those games out. She hated watching you go against your brothers on the ice."

I know the grin on my face is cocky as hell. "It's not my fault Leo and Hendrix couldn't get into the better hockey school."

Dad narrows his gaze in warning, and I laugh. "It'll be a good game. Tell her not to worry."

"Have you met your mother, son? She'll never stop worrying about you kids. So how about you tell me how you're really doing. Didn't look like Easton Hayes was too thrilled for you to be at the hospital benefit with his little sister the other night." He stands up, and Gordie pops right up with him.

Traitor.

I scoop the fat little fucker up and hold him in front of me. "You know you're mine, right?"

Dad chuckles and pulls a treat from his pocket, then holds it in front of Gordie's face.

No wonder he loves him. "You're bribing my dog."

"We used to bribe you kids too." Dad shrugs. "Works better on Gordie."

"Whatever . . . And to answer your question, Easton and I

are fine." Something about that doesn't ring true, but I keep that to myself.

"Didn't look fine, but suit yourself." He walks me to the front door but stops before he opens it. "You were always my kid that was the most focused, Nixon. Even more so than Gracie. She had her friends and a life apart from ballet. But you . . . you never let yourself have a life outside of hockey. It's been your whole life for as long as I can remember. Be careful. That's going to come back to bite you in the ass one day. Time is a thief."

"What do you mean?" I press because cryptic was never my thing.

"I don't want to see you looking back one day, wondering where it all went."

"How did you do it," I ask, honestly curious how he managed to balance it all. "How did you swing actually having it all? And how did you make it look easy? You and Mom have a solid marriage. You always made us kids feel like we came before football. And somehow you were still able to have a monster of a career. Seriously . . . if you'd have fucked something up, at least I'd have someone to blame my poor life choices on," I joke, but he just shakes his head.

"When you find the right person, you'll know. Wait for them. Because doing this life with your mother . . . the balancing act of it all. It was fun with her by my side. She kept me grounded. Find a best friend, Nixon. They make living this life so much better. But don't go searching. When the time is right, it'll happen. Trust that and follow your gut. Instincts are there for a reason, son. Listen to them."

That's twice he's said something like that. I guess he's getting less subtle these days. "I hear ya, Dad."

I don't tell him I heard him Saturday night too, even if I did.

I know he's talking about Kenzie because I don't typically

bring women around my family. I never have. But Kenzie's different, even if I'm not looking for anything long-term. But damn, do I want something with her right now.

NIXON

You delivering babies right now, doc?

KENZIE

If I was, I wouldn't be texting you back, now would I? I'm waiting on a stubborn baby girl who just isn't ready to be born yet. But she's coming soon, so I'm still at the hospital. What are you doing?

NIXON

Thinking about the other night on the phone.

KENZIE

Do you have any study sheets for me, Mr. Sinclair?

NIXON

You haven't had your next lesson yet. I've got to teach you the material before I can test you on it.

KENZIE

How about a course syllabus so I know what to expect?

NIXON

Let's just say our next lesson will consist of an oral quiz. Text me when you get home.

KENZIE

It could be late.

NIXON

I didn't ask what time, Mac.

KENZIE

Yes sir. Are you always so bossy?

NIXON

You have no idea, beautiful.

Kenzie

Chapter 14

I don't know how many coffees it takes to be considered a people person, but it's safe to say, it's not three.

—Kenzie's Secret Thoughts

It's close to midnight when I walk past Nixon's door and let myself into my own condo, only instead of being exhausted like I should be, I'm thinking about a certain sexy hockey player and his bossy demand that I let him know I'm home. My inner independent feminist is pretty sure I should have told him no one has told me what to do outside of an operating room in a long damn time. But I didn't . . . why didn't I? Oh, that's easy. Because it was fucking hot.

Why is everything he does such a turn-on?

I kick off my jeans, shoving them to the corner of my bedroom, and take in my reflection in the oversized, free-standing mirror propped up in the corner of the room. Standing here in a white, ribbed tank top and cheeky black panties, I don't look like much. The tan I worked so hard for during my break between residency and starting my job is fading. I've lost a few pounds I probably couldn't afford to lose. My boobs are pretty great though.

I turn to the side and smile at my reflection. My curves are more pronounced this way, and my ass might be small, but it's curvy. Definitely a solid handful.

I can't help but wonder what Nixon would think if he was standing here now.

Should I text him?

I pull my phone from my purse and look at the time staring back at me.

I mean, he did tell me to text him, and we're basically supposed to be each other's booty calls, right?

At least once we have sex, that's what we'll be.

Really, what's the harm in calling?

He's probably sound asleep with Gordie snoring at the foot of his bed.

I doubt he'll even wake up to see the text.

What can it hurt?

> KENZIE
>
> Just got home. Going to pour a glass of wine and go to bed. XOXO

I decide to delete the x's and o's. Seriously . . . who do I think I am, the *Kroydon Kronicles*?

> KENZIE
>
> Just got home. Going to pour a glass of wine and go to bed. Hopefully you're sleeping and this didn't wake you up.

There. That's better. I send that one off and grab a bottle of Riesling from my fridge and a wine glass from the cabinet. I'm alone with no one to judge, so I fill that bitch all the way up, grab mint chocolate chip ice cream from the fridge, and ask Alexa to play my favorite Eddie Vedder song. Ironically, the song is about seizing the day.

I slip my bra off and sing into my spoon as I dance around my kitchen in pink fuzzy socks, panties, and a tank. As the song slides into the next, my phone vibrates on the counter next to the bottle of wine.

NIXON

Let me in.

Oh shit. I guess he was awake.

Nixon

I hear music coming from the other side of the wall while I wait outside her door. Pretty sure I can hear her singing too. At least I can until I send my text. The singing stops then.

This woman is one giant contradiction. One I can't figure out, but I'm going to give it my best shot.

She's unbelievably beautiful but has no clue.

Sexy as hell, but she'd never believe it.

Brilliant but clumsy.

She says she doesn't want any strings . . . but this town would tie her down in a heartbeat if she let them.

And when she opens the door, all of that ceases to matter.

The building could burn down around us, and I'm not sure I'd notice or care.

"Mac . . ." I swallow and suck air in through my teeth. Fuck me.

Nobody should look that fucking hot in fuzzy fucking socks, but holy fuck, she does.

Her nipples are high, tight little points pressing against a white tank top, teasing me with a glimpse of the rosy-pink color visible beneath the fabric. One that's barely hiding what I'm absolutely positive will be the most magnificent breasts I've ever touched, and I'm going to touch . . . and taste . . . and fucking worship them.

I want to grab her face in my hands and kiss her.

Slam her up against the wall and fuck her.

But this is Mac, and that's not what we're doing.

Even if the sight of her has me ready to throw out every other rule I've ever had just to have her.

"Good fucking girl, Mac," I growl from deep within my chest as I step inside and kick the door shut behind me. "What do you have there?"

I nod toward the spoon in her hands. She licks it like a little brat and smiles. "My favorite ice cream. Do you want to try some?"

"Yeah, beautiful. I'm going to try some."

She blushes the prettiest shade of pink, and my mind goes in a million fucking directions.

She saunters by me with a swish of her hips, and I wonder where this boost of confidence came from and how I can harness it for her so she can always have it as I follow her into the kitchen. A small speaker sits next to a glass of wine and a carton of ice cream.

"You're fucking perfect, Mac." I lift her up and sit her on the island. "You ready for your next lesson?"

With wide eyes, she catches herself as she's about to nod, but then stops. "What does the lesson entail, Mr. Sinclair?"

I fucking love sassy Mac. "First, tell me where this is coming from. You seem different tonight."

I run my hands up and down her thighs and wait her out.

Mac's eyes trace the movements for a moment before her dazzling smile grows even brighter, and she flashes it right at me.

"You're so fucking beautiful."

She drops her hands on mine, stopping my movements. "I saved two lives today. There was a patient with a complication. The baby's heart rate was bottoming out. The mothers blood pressure was through the roof. So many things were going wrong all at once. It was chaos. But I knew what to do, and they're both alive tonight because of it. I didn't have to go into the waiting room and tell a husband that his wife and baby didn't make it. I got to tell him they're both going to be fine, and he has a healthy baby girl. I don't think there's a bigger high than knowing two people are alive thanks to me."

"That's amazing, Mackenzie," I tell her, awed.

I hit a puck into a net for a living, and this woman saves lives.

"Some days are really good days." She dips her spoon right into the carton of ice cream, then sucks the mint chip goodness right off it, giving me all sorts of ideas.

"I think a good day should be rewarded, don't you?"

She licks the ice cream off her lips and digs the spoon back into the carton, while slowly nodding her head.

Oh, I'm going to be using that spoon.

"Lie down, Mac." I can't even attempt to hide the need in my voice.

There's no hiding it. Fuck . . .

"What?" she squeaks, and there's my Mac, right back to her old ways. "I'm on the counter."

"Lie down," I tell her again, leaving no room for question, only this time she listens and leans back on her elbows.

Her tank rides up a few inches, baring a strip of her toned abs above her panties.

Her greedy gaze licks my skin. "You take your shirt off, Nix."

"You gonna accuse me of using steroids again?"

She shakes her head slowly and watches while I reach behind me and pull my shirt over my head. "What do you want tonight, Mac?"

"Umm . . . whatever you want to teach me," she murmurs.

"Not how this works. I need you to tell me what you want. The more vocal you are, the more I can give you what you need. The better this is for you. And this is all about you, beautiful. I want you to know just how good it can be with the right person."

She sucks in a breath. "And you think you're the right person?"

The idea of there ever being another person has me seeing a red mist in front of my eyes, but I don't tell her that. "I am tonight."

"I want your mouth on me." She hesitates and looks away. "And maybe my mouth on you," she adds, a little less sure of herself.

"Good girl. Now take off your shirt."

Again with those damn doe eyes that'll be the death of me. "But I'm not wearing a bra."

"Good, baby, because this is going to get messy." I scoop a spoonful of ice cream from the carton, then suck in my fucking breath when she peels her tank over her head, and my fucking God. There is nothing in the world more perfect than Mackenzie Hayes in nothing but black silk lace.

Fuck . . . My cock is leaking in my boxers.

"Say something, Nix . . ."

I want to say *mine*, but I can't.

That's not fair to either one of us.

"You're the most beautiful thing I've ever seen, Mac."

The flush that lights up her cheeks creeps down her chest, and I decide to follow it with the cool ice cream. I drag the spoon down her body, tracing her curves. Learning each one. Leaving a trail of cool, sticky sweetness that I lean in and lick off her neck. Her collarbone. The pulse point that's thrumming rapidly at the base of her throat.

When I look up, her golden eyes look lust drunk, and fuck if it's not a pretty look.

I dip my spoon back in the softening ice cream and love the way her back arches off the cool granite counter when I circle her tits—one, then the other, trailing lightly over her tight, pink nipples, eliciting a gasp as they harden even more.

Her belly trembles as I slide the ice cream over her toned stomach, dipping into her belly button, then licking it off her slowly. Savoring the taste of her skin and the tiny, jagged breaths leaving her lips.

"You doing okay, Mac?" I ask between sucking and licking and dragging more ice cream over her hip bones.

"Don't . . . Don't stop. Please," she manages to say before her hands reach down and grab my shoulders.

"Not a fucking chance, Mac."

"Oh, thank God," she whispers, and I smile to myself before I run the spoon along the edge of her black lace cheeky panties. The fabric covering her perfectly waxed pussy is soft and sheer, and fuck me . . . it's drenched.

She's so responsive, I want to rip them from her body.

But not yet.

I need to taste Mackenzie first.

Rather than ripping them off her like I want to, I run what's left of the ice cream over the lips of her pussy through the lace of her panties. This time, Mac's back bows off the counter, and her fingers tug at my hair as she moans my name.

I drop the spoon and push her thighs open.

Drunk off her taste and high off her smell, I throw her legs over my shoulders and drag my tongue up the length of her pussy through the lacy fabric.

"Ohh, just like that." she moans, and it's breathy and sexy and exactly what I want to hear from her. So I flatten my tongue and do it again. *And again*. And again.

I eat her through her soaked panties until she's a squirming, shaking, needy mess.

Until she's begging me for more and screaming my name.

My cock throbs in my pants as I finally rip the lace from her body and shove it in my pocket.

Her knees clamp tight against my head when I run a finger along the length of her sex, then slide it inside her, feeling her tighten around me. The sound she makes is mind-blowing, I unzip my pants and take my cock in my other hand and stroke myself as I feast on Mac.

The taste of her on my tongue is better than I could have ever imagined, and I fucking imagined this a lot over the years.

When I pull my finger out, she cries out from the loss until I trail it around her clit, just like she did the other night. "You like that, Mac? You like the way I fuck you with my tongue?"

She moans and tugs on my hair, trying to force me back where she needs me.

"Words, Mac." I quickly smack her pussy, and she moans as her body trembles beneath me.

"I fucking love the way you fucked me with your tongue. I love the way you licked me." I slide a finger back in, and she moans again. "And fingered me." I add another finger.

"What else do you want?" I growl, desperate for my own release.

"Pinch it . . . I want you to pinch my clit," she begs.

I lean down and suck her swollen little clit between my lips, then scrape my teeth over it and bite it just enough . . . and tug.

Mackenzie comes, screaming my name and soaking my face as I jerk my cock one final time, thinking I'll never get enough of her.

Kenzie

Chapter 15

Crying is not a sign of weakness.
Since the minute you were born it's been a sign of life.

—Kenzie's Secret Thoughts

ixon carries me into the shower after our lesson, holding me like the most delicate piece of fine china, and I let him. Probably another ding on my independent woman card, but I'll take the hit if it means I get to stay like this for a little longer.

I let him hold me. My body completely sated and relaxed, I surrender myself over to this foreign feeling. Relishing in it. And *maybe* enjoying that Nixon was the man to give it to me.

He stands me in front of the shower and turns on all six shower heads. Once he's satisfied with the temperature and the room fills with steam, Nix shoves down his jeans and boxer briefs, and my breath catches in my chest.

Nixon Sinclair is well-endowed.

I mean, he's big.

A god among men—massive, and *I* studied anatomy in

college, med school, and residency. I can safely say he's not the norm.

My initial thought is, *Holy shit, is that going to fit?*

But then my scientific brain kicks in, and I know it will fit. It'll just hurt like a bitch.

He cups my face in his hands and smirks. "Don't worry, beautiful. It will fit."

Shit . . . did I just say that out loud?

Nixon lathers my hair with shampoo and conditioner, then washes it out, massaging my scalp in the most delicious way. Not at all sexual but completely sensual.

I turn to face him, my eyes nearly as heavy as my thoughts.

It would be impossible not to feel this connection between us.

It's tangible, like corded steel wrapping around us, pulling us together, whether we want it or not.

I know I'm not supposed to want it.

I've worked my ass off for my career, and there just isn't room for anything else.

My heart beats rapidly in my chest as I remind myself there's a clock ticking on this thing with Nixon. There has to be. This isn't a relationship. This is using each other to scratch an itch. Someone else . . . someone less complicated with an easier job will come along and give him everything I can't.

Tick tock.

Falling hard for this man is going to be too easy, and heartbreak isn't on my bucket list.

The warm water soaks my skin and clings to my lashes as I look up at him and slowly drop to my knees. He might not be mine for long, but he's mine tonight, and I want more.

His strong body is cut like chiseled marble. Beautifully defined muscles cover golden skin. His dark hair sticks to his face, and those baby-blue eyes are dark . . . darker than I've ever seen them before. I'm not sure how I missed this all before coming home, but now that I've seen it, I'll never be able to look at him again without seeing him this way. He's like a god walking among mortals. A golden god.

"I think I'm ready for my next lesson, Mr. Sinclair."

I wrap my hand around his thick quads and look up through the pelting water. "I think it's your turn to tell me what you like. I've never done this before. So I think I need some help."

Is that really my voice?

Confident and sexy and wanting desperately to make him fall apart for me.

Needing to know I can give that to him.

His hand runs over my wet hair, and he wraps it around his fist, then tugs my head back. "This would be easier out of the shower, Mac."

"I'm not scared of hard, Nix."

"So fucking pretty on your knees for me." He tugs again. "Gorgeous."

When he says it like that, I believe him.

For the first time, that word doesn't make me self-conscious. It empowers me.

"This isn't a lesson, Mackenzie," he tells me with dark, hooded eyes. "This isn't for you to learn and use with anyone else. This is me showing you how I've wanted you to suck my cock for fucking years, Mac. You have no idea how long I've thought about your lips around my dick."

Oh. My. God.

My breath gets stuck in my throat, followed by a mouthful of water that I spit out.

"Open your mouth, beautiful." His grip on my hair tightens just enough to hurt the tiniest bit, and I press my thighs together, need pooling in my belly. Completely new sensations I can't get enough of.

He fists his erection, and I lick my lips in anticipation. "Wrap your hand around me."

I tentatively do as he says, barely able to wrap my hand around his thick cock.

He's huge.

I'm in medicine, and it feels ridiculously safe to say Nixon Sinclair has his fair share and everyone else's share too. My mouth waters, and I lean forward, needing to feel him in my mouth but waiting for his words.

"Put me between your lips . . ." I swirl my tongue around his crown, then take him between my lips and suck. "That's it, baby. Wrap your lips around me and take the first inch. Get used to it, because I want to fuck your face almost as much as I want to fuck that perfect cunt."

The warm, pounding water hides the red flush I have no doubt is covering my entire body. Not embarrassment. Not this time. No, this is all pure, unadulterated need. Need I never knew I could have.

"Good girl. Now take me deeper. Get it wet, baby. Don't worry about being sloppy. The messier, the better. But take it slow, Mac, because there's a lot of me to take, and if you're a good girl and take it all, the reward will be worth it."

Oh. My. Goodness. Yes, please. I want it all. Now. Like right now.

I work my way further down his shaft, loving that the pelting shower is covering us. Sheltering us. And hiding so many imperfections from my first time doing this. I hollow my cheeks and twist my hand, working him with both as I try to take him deeper. And my God, when Nixon's moan fills the fucking shower, I think I could come just from that sound alone.

"Fuck, Mackenzie. So good. Such a good girl for me."

I preen under his words and hands. He tugs on my hair, and I dig my nails into his ass. Who knew sucking dick could be so fun?

I slide further down, determined to take him down my throat and gag, my eyes watering. "Sorry," I murmur, and Nixon's eyes heat to two pools of molten blue fire.

"Fuck, yes. Don't apologize. You're doing so good, Mac. So fucking good."

I work my hand up and down his cock once, then twice, then take him back into my mouth and swallow while he holds my face. "Christ, Mac. That's it."

I look up through wet lashes, and Nixon throws his head back.

His muscles pulled tight.

Knowing I did this to him is such a turn-on.

"Tell me, Nix. Tell me what you like. Tell me what you want," I plead before licking his cock from base to tip and sliding my hand from his ass to cup his balls.

"You're doing so good, Mac. Twist your hands, suck my cock, and don't stop until you're swallowing my cum. Can you do that for me, beautiful?"

His praise lights me up, like he knows how to hit every hot button I never knew existed for me.

He lets go of my hair and pushes it out of my face before gathering it up again. "You okay if I'm a little rough?"

"God, yes," I moan as the rough pads of his fingers bite into my skin, and I take him back down my throat and swallow my gag as he fucks my face, shocked that I love it, but I abso-fucking-lutely do. I suck and lick and gag as I work him deeper and faster and harder, loving the sounds coming from Nixon. His words of praise.

I get high off each *good girl* that leaves his lips.

Each deliciously deep growl and moan.

His body tenses, but he's holding back, and that's not what I want.

"Don't stop," I plead, having had no idea how absolutely desperate I could be with the right partner. "I want it all, Nix. Give it to me, please."

"Fuck . . ." he groans, and I hum around him, feeling the vibration down to my core. My eyes go wide when the first line of hot, salty cum coats my tongue, but I don't stop. I hollow my cheeks and suck harder, working him faster, taking every last drop and wanting to please him like I've never wanted anything in my life.

After he gets his breathing back under control, Nixon bends down and lifts me in his arms like a groom carrying his bride over the threshold, and something inside me cracks. Maybe it's my heart. Maybe it's the wall around it I've spent years constructing. It's the smallest fissure, but it's there and scary as hell as he steps out of the shower and sets me on the vanity.

He wraps a fluffy towel around my shoulders and silently dries me, then himself before he picks me up again. "I can walk, Nix."

The whispered words feel rough on my swollen lips.

In truth, I'm spent. The adrenaline high has run its course, and exhaustion has taken hold, so I let him carry me. It feels good to be in his arms. Safe.

"I know," he tells me as he carries me into my bedroom and lies me down on my bed, then takes a step back. "I should go."

His voice holds something I don't recognize from him, but I can't place it, so I take a chance and grab his hand. "It's late. Why don't you stay?"

Nixon looks torn. "I shouldn't. You need your sleep, Mac."

I close my eyes and decide to give him a truth I don't

share often. "I don't sleep much, either way, Nix. It would be nice to not be alone."

I roll over, making room, and pull the blanket back. If tonight was about me taking control of my wants and needs, then I might as well ask for what I want, and what I want right now is to not be alone.

My breath hitches as he walks back into the bathroom, then comes back in, dressed in his boxers and carrying our clothes. "You want to be the big spoon or the little spoon?"

A giggle that sounds completely inappropriate in the quiet room slips from my lips. "I mean, I'm half your size, so the little spoon only makes sense, right?"

He lies down and wraps a hand around me, pulling my hips back and trailing his fingers up and down my ribs. "Why don't you sleep?"

I drag my nails over the arm tucked under my head, enjoying the way goosebumps break out over his skin.

And I wonder if the light of day tomorrow will make me regret the secrets I'm sharing in the quiet safety of tonight.

"I haven't slept well in years. Jules and Becks had me talk to a grief counselor about it when I was younger. I basically fear what will happen while I'm sleeping. What can change. What can be lost. It's something I've worked on over the years, and I can go a few months at a time without it being a problem, but when it starts again, I know I'm in for months and months with very little sleep."

He pulls me back against him, like his strength alone can keep my demons at bay. "Have you tried taking anything for it? My uncle uses melatonin to help him sleep."

I close my eyes and soak in the warmth of his body. The delicious way his fingers skim higher with each pass of my ribs. Just up high enough to touch the outer edge of my breast. It's soothing and sexy, and the need I felt in the shower sparks back to life. "I've tried everything. Herbal,

133

prescription, exercise, meditation. None of it really works, so most nights, I end up reading charts or studying. Throwing myself into medicine was a great excuse. There was always more studying to be done." I roll over in his arms and relish the way his eyes devour me.

"Basically . . ." I skim my fingers over his pecs and down his arms, tracing his Sinclair tattoo proudly inked into his gorgeous arm. "I look for anything to do to keep my brain occupied and hope that eventually exhaustion will set in."

Nix slides his knee between my thighs, that sexy smile back in place on his handsome face. "Anything . . . ?"

I nod my head and lick my lips. "Anything."

Nixon

Chapter 16

I don't know what I was thinking when I agreed to this *no strings attached* thing because lying here next to a naked, wet, vulnerable Mackenzie Hayes hits home just how much more than casual this woman will always be. It was never going to be any other way, and I'm pretty sure she and I are the only two people who didn't realize that.

Fuck me.

I want to tell her I'll always keep her safe, but she's not mine to make that promise to.

And if that doesn't rip me apart, nothing ever will

"What are you asking me for, Mac?" I cup the back of her head in my hand and stare down at her in amazement. Her pouty pink lips tip up in the corners, and the distance I thought I wanted to put between us by not kissing seems like the stupidest fucking idea I've ever had. Worse than no-strings sex with the one girl I always wanted.

Fucking fool.

"Show me, Nix. Show me how good it can be to not be alone. Give me that for a night."

Her words gut me.

For a night . . . We're not supposed to be more than a few nights strung together. But that's never going to be enough.

Her arms snake up my neck, and she pulls herself flush against me. "Do you have a condom?"

I swallow down my thoughts before they get any more out of control and press my lips against her forehead. "You sure, Kenzie?"

"Don't do that," she quietly snaps. "Don't put distance between us now. You told me to tell you what I wanted. Well, I'm telling you I want you to fuck me, Nixon." Her voice shakes, but she doesn't back down, and I swear to God the only sexier thing than her strength is her brain.

"Nix . . ." She presses her lips just below my ear and sucks and nips, and my cock definitely doesn't get the message that we're trying to be a fucking gentleman. "Please."

Please . . . That one word is all it takes to eviscerate me.

I flip her on her back and soak her in. "Fucking beautiful, Mac."

Her fingers run over my lips. "That's better. I don't like when you call me *Kenzie*. You only do that when you're not happy. Let's make each other happy, Nix. Show me how to make us both happy."

Christ.

I press my lips to her throat and suck, avoiding her lips.

If this is all we're going to be, we need a new fucking boundary.

Her pretty eyes drift shut, her lashes kiss her cheeks, and her lips part.

I take both her wrists in mine and pin them above her head, wanting to fuck her hard and fast and fucking raw until she's taken everything I have to give and begs me for more. But I can't. That's not what Mackenzie needs. What she deserves. Not this time.

There are a million ways I want to fuck this woman.

On her knees.

Bent over that goddamned island in the kitchen.

Straddling me, with her tits bouncing with each goddamn movement until she's screaming my name like a goddamn porn star. But that's not what tonight is about.

Tonight, she needs to be in control. She moans beneath me as she spreads her thighs, making room for my body. "You like that?"

"Mm-hmm," she murmurs as her eyes glaze over.

I lean down and grab my jeans from the floor, then fish a condom out of my wallet and slide it down my cock, only ever taking my eyes off her long enough to notice the over-sized, ornate mirror propped up in the corner of the room. "I want you to see what I see, beautiful."

"What?" she whispers in confusion before I pull her up in front of me and run my hands over her head and down her body, eliciting the sexiest shiver I've ever seen. It skips along her spine and stops at the twin dimples directly above her perfect heart-shaped ass. I run my hand over the soft skin, then smack one cheek, loving the bright red handprint it leaves. " So fucking beautiful."

Mac moans and looks over her shoulder at me, drunk with lust.

I bite down on her shoulder, then soothe the ache with my tongue. "I want you to watch us there, Mac." I point at the full-sized reflection of our bodies in front of us. "Don't turn around. Look straight ahead and watch me fuck you."

Kenzie

*N*ixon drags the head of his cock through my drenched sex, and the sight of him is almost as erotic as the feel of him . . . *So close.*

His big body dwarfs mine, and if I thought he looked like a god earlier, that didn't hold a candle to watching him like this. Seeing the need in his eyes. The way his chest rises and falls as his hands learn every inch of my body.

Caressing and teasing. Tweaking and spanking . . .

And my lord. *The spanking.* I have no words. Just needy, wanton desperation.

Nixon's golden skin looks sinful next to mine.

And if I knew sinning could be so sexy, I may have abandoned religion years ago.

His lips run along my shoulder, and his teeth graze over that sweet spot where my neck meets my shoulders, making my entire body vibrate.

His lips tilt into a sexy, self-satisfied smile as I shake, and he strokes my clit with his cock. "You ready for me, baby?"

It's the *baby* that does it for me.

I know it shouldn't. I have no right to want to be claimed by this man.

It shouldn't mean anything.

Doesn't mean anything.

But there's something about the possession in that single word that's intoxicatingly electrifying.

I watch as he notches his huge cock at my entrance, and my entire body quivers with anticipation.

He pushes in gently at first . . .

Just the tiniest bit before circling my clit with his fingers, then bringing them up to my mouth and painting my lips.

Without thinking about it, I lick my lips, and Nixon's dark pupils take over his entire eye as he stares at my mouth.

There's a war waging in those baby blues.

We stay there like that, frozen in time, for what feels like minutes but is actually only seconds. Standing still . . . until "Fuck it" is ripped from his lungs.

And finally, the kiss happens, like a bolt of lightning, violent and beautiful, stealing my breath from my chest.

On my gasp, Nix thrusts all the way inside me, and *oh God* . . .

Every single one of my senses rockets into hyperdrive.

Pleasure and pain spark and burst and tear at my body.

Agony and ecstasy claw at me in tandem.

Nix swallows my screams. "Such a fucking good girl," he praises against my mouth before his tongue sweeps inside. Tasting me. Teasing me. Fucking me into oblivion.

"Look at you taking me like such a good girl," he rasps against my mouth, and I gasp and watch our reflection long enough to feel the heat wash over every inch of my skin. His words leave me desperate for his praise.

"Yes . . . your good girl," I whisper and press my lips to his as he devours me.

Each stroke of his tongue against mine brings me higher . . . makes me hotter . . . until I'm soaring, and the pain no longer exists.

Nixon drags his thick cock out, and I whimper immediately at the loss before he pushes back in. Brushing against every inch of my tight walls. Ripping me apart in the sweetest way imaginable until I'm teetering on the sharp edge of a knife, sanity slipping into delirium. Unsure how much more I can take but wanting to take it all. Needing it. Begging for it.

My eyes stay glued to our reflection.

To the erotically beautiful sight in front of me and the way he's moving inside me but never taking his eyes from me.

It's not just Nixon. It's the way *Nixon* is watching me.

We're beautiful.

I can't look away. I refuse to.

A white, hot, electrifying pulse burns through me, threatening to destroy everything it touches. I moan and whimper until callused fingers grip my jaw, holding me still while Nixon's mouth takes mine again, and our tongues dance a wicked dance.

With each achingly slow stroke of his cock, his lips worship mine, soothing the pain until it's nothing but pleasure. Until my muscles contract around him. Stretching to take him deeper. Clawing to get him closer. Until we're moving in a savage harmony.

Pushing. Pulling.

Dying for more.

For everything.

"Tell me what you feel, Mackenzie." His raspy voice demands my submission, and my clit pulses as if his words are a physical touch.

"I feel . . ." I lick my lips and watch my chest rise and fall rapidly, entranced by our reflection. "Like every nerve . . . every synapse in my body is hypersensitive, and they're all lit up like the Fourth of July . . . Like I never want you to stop. Please God, don't stop."

Nixon grazes his teeth over my earlobe, then down my neck as he pulls out again, slower this time. Teasing me.

"Nix . . ." I keen.

He thrusts back in on the sexiest growl I've ever heard, then sets an unrelenting rhythm with each hard snap of his hips.

Fucking me harder.

Faster.

Forcing me to take it all, and God, I want it all.

Bringing me so close, I can taste my orgasm, then pulling back until it's just out of reach.

"Nix . . ." I cry. "I need . . ." I can't think. Can't speak.

Words fail me. Coherent thought fails me.

"Tell me, Mac. Tell me what you need," this beautiful man demands, and in his eyes . . . I can see myself through his eyes, and I like what I see. I look confident and sexy. Unafraid to take what I want and ask for more.

A strangled cry rips from my lips as he runs his hands over my breast and cups it in his palm. He pinches my nipple, and I feel it all the way down to the very center of my core.

"Yes . . ." I pant as my legs give out, and I drop my forehead down to the mattress.

I push my hips back, meeting him thrust for thrust before lights spark behind my eyes.

Nix soothes one hand over my ass and spanks me again.

A scream tears from my lips as lightning explodes behind my eyes. Violent flashes of color sizzle as I convulse around him, utterly destroyed.

Nix pulls out on a guttural roar, rips the condom off and strokes himself to an orgasm. Hot ropes of pearly cum cover my back before he collapses next to me and drags his finger through his orgasm.

"Open" he demands, and I open my lips in time for him to stuff two fingers inside my mouth. "Suck them clean, Mac."

Holy. Fucking. Hell.

Should this be hot?

Because . . . my God . . . so hot.

And as he rubs the rest of his cum all over my back, I can't stop thinking about how much I like it before he gets up. My eyes drift close until he comes back with a warm, wet washcloth and drops a kiss on my lips. "You passed with flying colors, Mac."

The last coherent thought I have is, *I guess maybe I wasn't broken after all.*

I was just waiting for Nixon Sinclair to come along and

ruin me for all other men.

Kenzie

Chapter 17

Behind every strong woman is a story that left her with two options.
Sink or fucking swim.
Floating through life isn't an option.

—*Kenzie's Secret Thoughts*

*buzzing pulls me from my sleep, followed by a husky voice. "Mac . . ."

I bury my face in my pillow, not ready for my dream to be over yet. My dreams never seem this . . . *live action.* I can feel Nixon's weight on me, and it feels divine. I don't want it to disappear, so I struggle to hang on to the last threads of sleep.

The buzzing won't stop.

"Baby, I think your phone is ringing."

Baby . . . ? What the—

I pop my eyes open and realize Nixon's weight feels so real because it is very real and very much wrapped around me. "That wasn't a dream?" I ask hoarsely and lick my dry lips.

"Shit. That wasn't a dream." I fly out of bed, looking for my pager. "Where's my—"

Nixon sits up, shirtless, and grabs something from my nightstand.

I do not need to be noticing the way his muscles flex in the early morning light.

I swallow down that thought as he hands me my pager and phone. "Thanks," I murmur. "Shit." I hit speed dial and lock my eyes with Nix. "Brynnie thinks she's in labor."

Deacon picks up on the first ring. "Kenzie . . . Brynn's water just broke. I'm putting the phone on speaker. She's getting dressed."

Shit. She's nearly three weeks early. "Sounds like we're having a baby today. Is she contracting?"

"*She* can hear you," Brynn snaps from what sounds like across the room. "And I thought they were Braxton Hicks."

I realize I'm standing in the middle of my bedroom, completely naked, and Nixon is just sitting there staring at me with hungry eyes, and my stomach flips.

Damn. That's going to take some getting used to.

"How far apart are the contractions?" I ask, knowing her answer will determine whether I get to shower or not.

"Umm . . ." Brynn waffles, and I hear Deacon whispering sweet words to her.

"They've been about eight minutes apart," he tells me, and Brynn clears her throat and groans.

Yeah. That's definitely another one.

Once she can speak again, she moans. "More like six minutes, Kenz."

"Six minutes," Deacon blurts out, and she shushes him.

"I didn't want to worry you. I thought we had at least three more weeks."

"Red." His voice is soft and placating. "You're bag's

packed. Let's go. Anything you don't have, someone can grab."

I look at the clock. "Nope. No more packing. I want you to grab what you have and head to Kroydon Hills Hospital. I'll meet you there."

Looks like no shower for me.

"Shit," Deacon chokes.

"What's wrong?" My radar goes on high alert. This is the first time I'm delivering a loved one's baby, and I'm going to make sure everything goes right for her. It has to.

"I've got to wake Kennedy up. Jace and India aren't home," he groans.

Deacon's assistant coach is Brynnie's and my Uncle Jace, and he happens to live next door to them. But he and his wife left this morning for her brother's wedding.

See . . . ? Six degrees of Kevin Bacon.

"I can take her," Nixon offers, and all the color drains from my face as the other end of the line goes silent . . . Until it isn't.

Damn it.

"Kenzie . . ." Brynnie says calmly. Too calmly. "Why do I hear Nixon's voice in your condo at four-thirty in the morning?"

"That's not Nix," Deacon tries to tell her, but he's full of shit. Not only has he coached Nixon for a handful of years with the Revolution, he also coached Nixon at Boston University before that. That man knows the voice of the man I slowly turned to glare at.

"Don't bullshit a bullshitter, dear. Oh, fuck this." She must take the phone from Deacon because her voice gets much closer and clearer through the call. "Nixon Joseph Sinclair. What are you doing with her at four a.m.?"

"Brynlee," Deacon tries to calm her, but she's just getting started.

145

"All of you shut up, or I will refuse to go to the hospital, and you'll have to deliver the baby here. Now, someone tell me why Nixon is with you if you two are fake dating— because that doesn't sound fake to me."

Deacon coughs, and Nixon laughs as I slide on a pair of panties and grab a fresh pair of jeans. "Pretty sure you know what he was doing there, babe."

I silently cringe.

He's taking his life in his own hands, talking to a laboring woman like that.

"Fine. But if we spend hours waiting for this baby to come, I want every dirty detail, Hayes. And as for you, Sinclair. How fast can you get to our house? Kennedy loves you. She'll be fine staying with you . . ." She pants and groans as another contraction hits her.

"Nope, Deacon. Wake Kennedy up. Bring her in her pajamas. Grab whatever she needs, and we'll set her up in a room with Nixon until someone else can come and take her home. You are leaving now. It sounds like you're in active labor. Do not pass go, and get your ass to the hospital. I'll meet you there in fifteen minutes."

"What?" she cries, and I can hear the tears in her voice. "Kenz . . ."

"You're going to be fine, Brynlee. Just get moving, and I'll be right there. Love you," I tell her as I throw on a long sleeve t-shirt and my brother's Revolution hoodie with his name and number on the back.

"Love you too, Kenz."

She hangs up, and I look at Nix, who's still just sitting on the edge of my bed, deliciously naked. He's impressive, and he's not even erect.

Wait. I'm mad at him.

"Couldn't help yourself, could you?" I ask as I walk into

the bathroom, put on deodorant, and throw my hair up into a bun. "*Had* to offer to take Kennedy."

I brush my teeth quickly and swish some mouthwash as he walks in behind me.

He's in his jeans, shirtless.

Oh yeah. That's probably because his shirt is still in the kitchen.

Nixon picks up my toothbrush and shakes his head when I make a sound of protest. "That's my toothbrush," I groan, and the way he looks at me has me thinking thoughts I don't have time for.

Nix brushes his teeth, spits it out, then backs me up against the bathroom vanity. His lips ghost over mine. "My mouth was all over every inch of your body last night. It was inside your body. You really want to complain about me using your toothbrush?"

Why does his nearness take my breath away?

I definitely don't have time to figure that out now.

I dig my fingers into the hair that needs a cut at the nape of his neck and kiss him hard and fast. "I guess when you put it that way, I'll forgive you for that. But I swear to God, Nix. You just opened Pandora's fucking box by letting Brynnie know you're here. We're going to have to talk about this later."

He runs the tip of his finger across my hairline and tucks an uncooperative curl behind my ear. "Let them talk, Mac. You need to go be a rockstar, and I get to hang with the coolest kid I know that I'm not technically related to. You know Kennedy. She wouldn't be comfortable with just anyone."

I shake my head. "We have a bajillion family members who live in that neighborhood." I duck under his arms and dart into my room to grab my shoes and purse. "She could have gone to any of their houses, Nixon."

He shrugs, and a slow, sexy, mischievous smile spreads across his face. "Let's go, Hayes. I'll drive."

"I need my car, Nixon. I'm going to be there all day," I protest as we walk into the kitchen, and he throws on last night's shirt. Surprisingly, it's still clean. Not a drop of mint chocolate chip to be seen.

Fuck . . . he's so sexy.

"Are you on call or just delivering Brynnie's baby?" he asks as he holds open my condo door for me.

"I'm not on call again until Wednesday," I tell him, remembering one of the main reasons he and I can't possibly work. We'll never see each other.

"Then I'm driving, and I'll drive you home. Let me in your world a little, Mac."

He drops a hand to my lower back as we step on the elevator, then backs me into the corner and runs his nose up my neck. "I might surprise you, beautiful."

You already have, Nixon.

You already have.

Nixon

I look over my cards and across the table, in the private waiting room the nurses set Kennedy and I up in hours ago, and study my opponent. It might be harder to read her if I hadn't known her since she was five. "I think you're bluffing, kid."

"Care to make a bet?" She holds up a chocolate bar.

I pull out the contents of my pockets. I've got fifty bucks, a half a pack of gum, my phone, and my keys. I move the gum to the center of the table, and she eyes the money in my hand instead. "Not a chance, kid."

"Can't blame a girl for trying." She yawns, and it reminds me of how young she still is. "How much longer do you think it'll be?"

Cade St. James, Brynn's dad, walks in and hands me a cup of coffee. "Could be a while, Kiki. Babies don't like timelines.

"You want me to take you home? We could wait there," I offer, and she shakes her head.

"I want to be here when he's born. Dad said I could be the first person to see him." She drops her cards and tugs her blanket around her, then closes her eyes. "He also made me promise not to tell Scarlet that."

Cade chuckles. His wife, Scarlet, is a force to be reckoned with.

Nobody tells her what she can and can't do.

"Yeah well, you're the big sister. Scarlet understands that, kiddo," he tells her as he drops down into the seat next to her. "Take a nap. We'll wake you up when there's news."

We sit in a comfortable silence until a small snore leaves Kennedy's lips. As if that was what was holding back the incoming interrogation, Cade's eyes narrow on me. He might be a retired MMA champion, having passed on his title to his brother-in-law, and now years later, his son, but swear to God, I wouldn't want to piss him off or hurt someone he loves. He's definitely still capable of fucking a man up.

"So where's Scarlet?" I ask, knowing she's not far. My mom and she are good friends. I know Brynn's family well.

Cade leans back and crosses his arms over his chest. "She's in the hall, talking to Becket and Jules."

Fuck.

"What's wrong, Nix? You're looking a little pale there. You feeling all right?" Cade pushes. Guess Mac was right, and word's already getting around.

The door to the private waiting room opens again, and

out of the corner of my eye, I catch Becket and Maddox's dad, Sam, walking in, each with a coffee in their hand. I've heard stories over the years about how close these three are.

The former MMA champ, the US Senator, and the mob boss.

It's like the start of a bad joke.

"Care to tell me why you were the one who drove Kenzie in this morning, Nixon?" Becket asks calmly, and I bite my tongue. He doesn't scare me.

"She needed a ride," I offer politely, even though he's eyeing me up like I just defiled his little girl. Which I did. A whole fucking lot. In many, many ways. I also want to do it again. And again. I want to spend months buried inside Mackenzie Hayes.

"Should I make a joke about *riding* the way you cracked all the jokes when Deacon came home with Brynn, you asshat?" Cade asks with a glacial glare over the rim of his stale, tasteless hospital coffee.

"Please don't," Becket groans, and again, I keep my mouth shut.

I have no clue what the fuck I'm supposed to say.

I don't have any clue what the fuck I'm even supposed to say to *her*, let alone to these three.

"You're not going to add anything, Prince?" Becket asks Sam, who groans.

"Listen, you smug fuck. I still have a daughter who's going to fall in love with some young asshole one day, and I'm not stupid enough to think you two won't be there to make it worse. So I'll save all my comments for *this* young asshole instead of throwing them at you." He levels me with a stare that could make a man piss his pants. It would probably work too, if I hadn't grown up spending the night at his house every few weekends. His wife saved my mom's life when she was pregnant with the twins.

Fuck.

Our families are so intertwined.

Mac and I getting together is either the stupidest thing I've ever done or it was inevitable.

I don't believe much in fate, but I'm going with option two.

I wait for one of them to say something . . . anything.

But they don't, they just all sit and wait until I crack.

Doesn't take too long. "I think I'm going to go check on Mac . . ."

"She's busy," Becket tells me, and Sam chuckles but doesn't say anything. "You might as well say it. I know you're thinking it."

"I'm not thinking anything," Sam tells him, then looks my way. "Unless you want to tell him what she was busy doing before coming to the hospital, Nix?"

Cade chuckles, and I stay quiet.

"Just don't hurt her, Nixon." Becket clears his throat. "She's a good girl with a big heart and a fucking ton of hurt already weighing her down. She doesn't need someone to add to that. *Understand?*"

I look him in the eyes and ignore everyone else in the room. "Respectfully, if things are going to go anywhere with Mac and me, that deserves to be a discussion between her and me, not me and the three of you. But I can tell you I respect her. I've cared about her for half my life, and I'd never hurt her or let anyone else hurt her. I'm not sure what you're asking. But that's what I can tell you right now."

"Quiet confidence is a good thing, Nixon. You've always had that. Remember that," Sam tells me with a small nod of his head, while Becket just sits, staring at me, apparently trying to decide what he wants to say.

"You gonna speak, Becks, or can he go now?" Cade asks.

"Keep her safe, Nixon," Becket warns.

"I'd protect her with my life, Becket." And I mean every fucking word.

Scarlet opens the door with a beautiful smile on her face and tears pooling in her eyes. "He's here." She walks over and wakes up Kennedy. "Your brother is here, and they're asking for you."

Kennedy stretches and moves next to me. "Will you walk me down, Nix?"

"Sure." I kiss Scarlet's cheek and nod at the men gathered in the room. "Congratulations."

And minutes later, when Kennedy opens the door to Brynlee's room and I lock eyes with Mackenzie, it clicks. My heart feels like it's going to thrum right out of my chest.

She's holding Brynn's baby, and I know without a doubt in my fucking mind, that woman right there is mine. One day, this will be us. She'll be holding our kids, and I'll be the happy fucker in the corner of the room, helping his wife, like Deacon is helping Brynn get adjusted in the bed. He embraces Kennedy, and as she walks over to Brynn, he mouths *thank you* to me. And I wonder if I should be telling *him* that.

"Do you want to meet him, Nix?" Brynlee asks quietly, and I shake away my quickly firing thoughts and get a little choked up. Brynlee might not be my sister, but I've known her my entire life, and unlike Mac, I've always looked at Brynn like one of my sisters.

"You sure, Brynn? I don't want to interrupt. I should leave," I stammer.

"Come in, Sinclair. This is probably the calmest it's going to be for days," Deacon tells me, exhaustion and elation lining every inch of his face. "Meet our son, Knight."

I step inside, and Mac moves next to me, holding the tiny baby boy wrapped in a pale blue blanket. "He's perfect," I say as all other words escape me. "Welcome to the world, Knight."

I don't touch him. Just watch in awe. Taking it all in for a moment.

Then I look up at Mac's beautiful face and tuck that same curl from earlier behind her ear. "You're a rockstar, Hayes."

Fuck. This is it. This is that thing Dad always talks about. That moment when you just fucking know, and it all changes.

She smiles softly, and Bryn laughs. "Hey. I'm the one who just pushed a ten-pound, two-ounce watermelon out of my vagina, Sinclair. Kenzie just spent hours yelling at me to push."

Mac gasps softly, careful not to wake the sleeping baby as she carefully hands him off to his mother. "I did not yell at you."

Brynn grabs Mac's hand and squeezes, and a sob catches in her throat. "Thank you for being here for me, Kenzie. I can't imagine doing this with anyone else."

"Hey, what am I?" Deacon jokes, and Brynn shakes her head.

"You are my everything, my love."

He kisses her head, and I feel like an intruder at this moment. As the room quiets, I move next to the bed and kiss the top of Brynn's head. "You did so good, Brynlee. He's beautiful." Then I turn and shake Deacon's hand. "Congratulations, Coach."

"Take our girl home, Sinclair," Brynn whispers, never looking away from her son.

Our girl. Yeah . . . I'll share her with the girls. But part of me wants to tell her she's *my* girl. Guess I'm going to have to convince Mac of that first.

"I'm going to catch a few hours of sleep, but I'll stop by later today to check on you, okay?" Mac tells her, then follows me out of the room. "Any chance I can take you up on that ride, Sinclair? I'm exhausted and need a nap."

"Any chance there's room in your bed for me?" I ask, not ready to say goodbye. I know she's not ready to hear what I want to say, so for now, I'll have to settle for her not being ready to say goodbye either.

Mac comes to a sharp stop, and all joking vanishes. "I slept better last night than I can remember sleeping in years. You can be my bed buddy whenever you want."

I run my hand over her hair and squeeze the back of her neck. "Be careful, Mac. I might just take you up on that."

She leans her forehead against mine, eviscerating any distance either of us has been trying to cling to. "Good."

A throat clears behind us, and I half expect a Kingston to be standing there. Only it's not one of the many. I look up to find Dr. Dick standing beside us, clearly annoyed. More than that, he looks angry. Douchebags never like it when you take something they think is theirs, even if they never had a claim to it. And this asshole has no claim on this woman and never will.

"Dr. Hayes. And Mr. Sinclair." His words are curt and unimpressed. "I'd hope you could be more professional while you're working, Dr. Hayes."

"What the—" I start but clamp my lips closed when Mac places her palm on my chest.

"Sorry about that. I was actually just leaving, Dr. Richardson."

He looks her over like he's seeing her in sexy lingerie instead of pink scrubs, and I don't like it. This dude gives me a bad fucking feeling.

"Don't let it happen again, Dr. Hayes," he warns before he walks off, and I clench my fist at my side.

"There's something wrong with him, Mac. I don't like him," I tell her as she pulls me behind her into a room marked *Attending's Lounge*. She moves in front of a locker and expects me to be able to think while she changes her clothes.

"You don't need to like him or tolerate him. I do. And I'm hoping that between seeing whatever he just saw and seeing us together at the event, maybe he'll take the hint and back off."

Once she's changed, she snaps her fingers in front of my face. "Earth to Nixon. You still with me, Nix?"

I grip her hips and pull her toward me. "You can't strip in front of me and expect me to be able to form sentences, beautiful."

She beams back at me.

"So fucking beautiful."

And so fucking mine.

Yeah . . . I like the sound of that.

This time, I leave it be while I drive us back to our building and hold her while she sleeps soundly for hours. *Mine.*

HOCKEY HELL

Are the Revolution boys falling apart at the seams?
Kroydon Hills's favorite hockey team played their last three
preseason games this week, and they lost each one. This isn't
the team we're used to seeing.
Rumors are swirling about infighting between the team.
Could the magical era of Philadelphia hockey be coming to
an end? Stay tuned and see . . .

#KroydonKronicles #HockeyHell

Nixon

Chapter 18

*E*aston storms out of the locker room after a shit practice, and Leo whistles as he watches him go. "What's the matter with him? He finally find out where Goldilocks has been sleeping?"

"Christ. You're an idiot. You know that, right? Get your shit together, and try to take it seriously, brother. Game one is next week." I lace up my boots and shut my locker. "Wait . . . am I Goldilocks in this scenario?" I ask and smack the back of his big head.

"I *am* serious. You didn't see *me* fucking up out there. I'm not pulling fouls and looking sloppy as shit. I've got my shit on lockdown. I'm also not the one secretly fucking around with my team captain's little sister. You might want to look in the mirror before you call me stupid, shithead."

"He's the fucking co-captain," I mumble under my breath, wishing I were sleeping with her, but that would mean I've seen her. And it's been almost a week since I've set eyes on Mackenzie Hayes.

A fucking horrible week. We've lost each game we've played, and the domino effect it seems to have had on the team has been massive. It's like someone picked at a tiny thread, and now we're unraveling at the seams.

Coach is distracted. Brynnie's blood pressure sky-rocketed while she was in the hospital, so they ended up keeping her a few extra days. Coach is running ragged between the hospital, home, and here.

Our left winger fractured his arm in two places in a drunk driving accident Monday night with our backup goalie driving. The press has been all over us. Management has been all over us. It's mind-blowing how one fucking week can change a team's dynamic.

Leo shuts his locker and looks over at the Wilder brothers. "You guys want to grab lunch?"

We try to do lunch with Everly and Gracie's husbands once a week after practice. Easton joins us most of the time. But no one looks like they're in the mood today.

"Nah, man." Ares checks his phone. "Gracie hasn't been feeling great. I'm heading home."

"Same. Everly closed the shop early today." Cross smiles, and I gag a little.

"Dude. I don't need to hear what you two are doing when she cuts out of work early," Leo adds, and I see it on his face before he says anything else, so I slam his hockey bag into his stomach, stopping the impending verbal vomit that'll absolutely include something about Mac and me.

I gotta get my own place. He's killing me.

"Come on, shit for brains." I clap his back and move him along. "Callen is waiting for us at West End." I shove him through the locker-room door and outside into my truck. "Seriously, man. What's wrong with you? Are you trying to get me killed?" I ask, pissed off.

Tensions are too high, and he's been pulling this shit all week.

Saying dumb shit whenever he can. *Stirring the pot.*

"Dude. You can't keep denying it. You might as well get it out there," he tells me, and if it were anyone else, I'd have beaten the shit out of him on the ice already.

I look at him from the corner of my eye as my knuckles turn white with my hold on the steering wheel. "Did Mom drop you on your head as a baby or something?"

"You probably did it yourself because you didn't want to share, dickhead," he groans. "I'm trying to help you, man. You've been fucking miserable all week, and you're constantly checking your phone. Quit sneaking the fuck around and start dating her in public. Kenzie's hot as fuck. I don't get why you're hiding it. You ashamed or something?"

It takes everything I have not to slam on the breaks and hope he hits his head on the dashboard. "You really do need help, brother. Mac has been on call every night this week. She's covering for a colleague at a hospital in Philly. We're not hiding anything because there's nothing there to hide. I've barely talked to her, and we're figuring things out. Stay the fuck out of it, Leo. Seriously, man. I'm telling you to stop."

Figuring things out might be a little strong.

I've got no fucking clue where her mind is.

I know where mine is, but even that isn't as easy as it sounds.

We came back from the hospital last weekend, stripped down to our underwear, and just slept for hours. She never set her alarm, so she slept through dinner with her family and shocked the hell out of me when she wasn't at all worried about it. She shot a text off to Juliette, and that was that. We went back to bed.

That time, we did more than sleep.

She insisted there's more she wants to learn, and I was happy to be the one *teaching* her. But I haven't seen her since I left her on Sunday, and Leo isn't wrong. I'm fucking agitated. I want to see her, but I get the pressures of her job, and I'm not going to add to it. Even if we need to talk.

"You want me to be serious? Okay, this is me serious. You're hiding all kinds of shit, brother, and Kenzie is the only thing I've called you out on. Why is Hunter calling? Why the hell are you ignoring him?"

I look down at my phone in the center console and see Hunter's name flashing on the screen *again*.

"You got something you want to share, brother?" Leo pushes, pissed off. "Cause things aren't adding up. You've had a thing for Kenzie Hayes since we were kids. Why aren't you locking that shit down? She's incredible. She's smart and hot and could give a shit who your family is because hers makes ours look like underachievers. And that's saying something. Now Hunter's been trying to reach you for weeks, and you're ignoring him . . ."

I pull into West End and turn off the car. "It's not—"

"Don't bother lying, Nix. Hunter called me yesterday and asked me why the hell you haven't called him back. He wouldn't break confidentiality, but seriously, man, I know you. And this shit isn't adding up." Leo doesn't get angry. He's always been the easiest-going brother. He lets everything roll off his back and likes to mask it all with humor. But right now, he's fucking pissed, and he's not wrong.

"Listen . . ." Leo looks at me like he knows what I'm about to say, and he probably does. "The weight of it all has been getting to me. That's all."

The look on his face says it all.

Disappointment and distrust.

Not two things Leo, Hendrix, and I usually feel toward each other.

"Do you ever worry about letting Dad down?" Jesus, I'm pushing fucking thirty, and I'm bitching about my daddy issues.

He drags his hand over his face and looks away. "Dude. How the fuck are we not supposed to worry about that? His jersey hangs in the Hall of Fame."

"Not just athletically. Just . . . I don't know. Like the man you are. The priorities you have. Dad made it all look easy, and the only thing I ever remember him asking of us was to always give 110 percent to whatever we were doing." My gut churns at the thought.

"Earn it," we both mumble in unison, having heard it so many times throughout our lives. If it's worth doing—worth having— you need to earn it. Nothing is given to you.

"Nix, you're always one of the first ones at practice and one of the last ones to leave. You work harder than everyone, including me. What the hell are you worried about? That Dad will be disappointed?" he asks, and it sounds ridiculous.

"I don't know, man. I just don't want to throw away what he gave us. We've got this great family and great lives here. But I'm not gonna lie, it was nice being in Boston. I liked not having the shadow of the Sinclair legacy hanging over my shoulder every day. Perfect family. Perfect relationship. Perfect fucking career. He handled it all like it was nothing, and some days . . . it's just a lot." I stop when Callen pulls his massive truck into the spot next to ours.

"I mean, I guess when you put it that way, it is. But honestly, Nix, you've always been an overthinker, and I think you're doing it now." Callen knocks on Leo's window, and Leo gives him the finger. "Mom and Dad had their own hell to go through to get here. They just want us to be happy. Whatever the hell that looks like."

Callen knocks again.

"Fuck off, Uncle," Leo yells before he looks at me again. "Even if that means leaving Kroydon Hills."

Guess my little brother is more observant than I gave him credit for.

KENZIE

Dr. Dick just asked me if you and I were still together and if I could get him tickets to a Philly Kings game.

NIXON

Does he think you can get him tickets because I'm related to the coach?

KENZIE

I think so.

NIXON

Does the dumb fuck not realize you're related to the team owners?

KENZIE

I'm not sure.

NIXON

What did you tell him about us?

KENZIE

I didn't. I glossed right over it. Then he asked about the game and mentioned maybe we could go together. I don't think he has any concept of propriety.

NIXON

Are you on call tonight?

KENZIE

I am. It's my last night. Why? Have you written your next lesson plan?

NIXON

I thought it could be more like a hands-on assignment. Why don't you come over after you're done?

162

KENZIE

It could be late.

NIXON

I'll be awake.

KENZIE

Okay. I'll text you when I leave.

NIXON

And Mac – plan on spending the night.

Kenzie

Chapter 19

I'm not like other girls.
I know what I want for dinner.
I've been thinking about that shit since lunch.

—*Kenzie's Secret Thoughts*

"*D*r. Hayes." I stop and take a deep, *not at all calming* breath before I turn around to answer Dr. Dick.

Twice in one day.

Aren't I just a lucky duck?

Who the hell came up with that phrase anyway?

Why are ducks lucky?

The cute little guys have to swim like crazy just to stay afloat. Their little feet are going a mile a minute under the water, working hard as hell. Maybe it's because while all of that is going on, they still look calm, cool, and in control. Holy shit. Do I envy a duck?

"Good evening, Dr. Richardson."

"Are you heading out?" he asks as he looks me over, disdain remaining in his expression where a moment ago, there was something else.

I ended up with vomit on my dress today because why not end an extremely long week that way. I changed into my spare clothes and threw on my Hayes Revolution hoodie. Not exactly what I'd call hospital appropriate, but I'm leaving, not working. And I swear to God, if he gives me shit, I'm either going to nut-punch him or cry. It could go either way.

I smile sweetly and hope for the best because seriously, my give-a-fuck meter isn't operating at full capacity at this point this week. I haven't slept for more than a handful of hours in days. "I am."

I stop myself from saying more because he doesn't get to know anything else.

Why would I tell him how tired I am. Or that the last time I got a good night's sleep was when I spent the night in Nixon's arms. And he absolutely doesn't get to know how desperately I want to be back there with him again.

Dr. Dick places his hand at the small of my back, and my skin crawls. When the right man does this, it's calming. When *this* man does this, icky is the only highly educated word that comes to my mind. "Why don't I walk you out, Mackenzie?"

I step forward, out of his touch, and angle my body away from his. "Oh, that's all right." I pull my phone from my pocket, ready to act like I have to call Nixon or Becket or anyone who can remind this man that he's the last man I would ever look to in my life. But I'm saved from resorting to that tactic when Bellamy skips down the final few stairs. Her jacket is on, and her bag is over her shoulder.

Relief washes over me. "Hey Bellamy," I wave her over. "You ready to leave?"

She looks from Dr. Dick to me and moves into my side. "I am. You ready?"

"Yes." I breathe a sigh of relief. "Have a nice night, Dr. Richardson."

Bellamy and I walk out together without looking back, but Dick's eyes burn into me the whole time.

"Are you okay, Kenzie? You look a little . . . off."

There's a crisp chill in the air tonight. A definite marker of the changing of the seasons. Goodbye, summer. Hello, fall. I feel like I may have lost a season sometime over the past week.

The moon is full as we walk toward the employee parking lot, but there's still not enough light, and I'm so relieved I didn't have to walk out here with Dr. Dick. "I swear he's getting bolder. He asked me about going to a football game earlier and put his hand on my back before you came over." I try to shake off the disturbing feeling.

This man's sense of entitlement is escalating.

"Maybe you should tell someone, Kenzie. It would be very different coming from you than from other people. Your aunt is a well-respected doctor at the hospital, and so are you. And let's not forget that your word will carry more weight than a nurse's would. It's a shitty fact, but that doesn't make it less true."

It is a shitty fact.

One we need to work on fixing.

"Maybe . . . I'll think about it." I point toward my car. "I'm parked over there. Where are you?"

She nods in the opposite direction. "Are you off this weekend? We're having a watch party for Callen's game Sunday night."

"I am. No on-call for the next five days," I tell her without saying I'll be there.

"You should come. It'll be fun." When I don't answer, she smiles and shakes her head as she starts to walk away. "I know where you live."

"I'll try," I offer to appease her, and she laughs.

"Yeah . . . We'll see."

Right now, I can only think as far as getting to Nixon and whatever he has in store for our next lesson. And the sleep that will come after.

KENZIE

Just pulled in. You still feel like company?

NIXON

Company? No. You? Always.

KENZIE

Good answer, Sinclair. I bet you say that to all the girls.

NIXON

How about you get that perfect little ass up here and let me show you just how many girls I want in my life, Mac.

Shit. That just took a turn I'm not ready for.

Maybe this isn't a good move.

But as the elevator doors open on my floor, I'm drawn to Nixon's door, not mine. Only hesitating for a moment before I knock tentatively. Gordie's excited bark welcomes me just before Nixon opens the door.

His hair is messy, like he's run his hands through it a few times, and I itch to do the same. A tight black tank hugs his chest and proudly displays each beautiful muscle, and gray sweatpants hang from his lean hips. Hips I want to lick. Hips I want to feel pressed against me.

"Hi," I whisper and stand frozen for a moment as electricity arcs between us, sparking and soaring like a live wire being drug along the street.

Pretty to look at but so damn dangerous to touch.

We're irresistibly drawn together by an invisible force.

And right now, I just don't have the energy to fight.

I'm not sure who reaches first. My arms circle his neck as Nixon lifts me from my feet and moves me inside. He leans me against his front door, and I wrap my legs around his waist as his mouth devours mine. "Fucking missed you, Mac."

Those words. God, they shouldn't have this effect on me, but they really do.

Our tongues tangle as we get completely lost in the moment.

Just us and this kiss that somehow shatters my world as I cling to this man.

He pulls back and presses his forehead against mine. "You okay, baby?"

Damn him.

Tears pool in my eyes, and the weight of the week pushes me over my limit.

Nixon swipes his thumbs under my eyes and carries me into his bedroom.

"I don't even know where this is coming from. I'm not a crier." I sniff.

He sits down on the bed with me in his lap. "It's been a hell of a week, Mac. I'm sure everything with Brynn was weighing on you. And I can only imagine how many hours you've worked. Plus, that shit with Dr. Dick. It's a lot. How about you let me take care of you? Maybe get a little sleep."

"I'm sorry." Guilt tugs at me because what he's proposing sounds perfect. "You're not supposed to be taking care of me, Nixon. You're supposed to be teaching me." I know I'm throwing up walls, but this overwhelming need mixed with such a sense of safety . . . Of *more*. It scares the hell out of me.

"Part of teaching you is making sure you know how you deserve to be treated. Sleep, baby. There's plenty of time for everything else. Just do me one favor."

Nixon's hands slide under my shirt and skim up my sides. "Arms in the air, Mac."

I lift my arms over my head, wondering where in the world he's going with this until he strips the hoodie and shirt off my body, then sits me on the bed as he stands and steps into his closet. He comes back out holding an old Boston University hockey tee that he slides down over my body. "When you're in my room, you wear my name."

A weary, watery smile tugs at my lips at that deviously possessive tone I've come to love. And as if that thought alone wasn't enough to send me running for the hills, he squats down in front of me, unties my sneaks, and pulls them and my jeans down my legs and off my body. He drags his lips up my calves and presses them against the inside of my thigh before pulling back the heavy down comforter and sliding my legs under it.

Heavy eyes hold my gaze hostage, while a sliver of moonlight filters through the shade, and a cool breeze blows in from the open window. His room smells like a fall night mixed with a warm fire. It's heat and spice and everything Nixon Sinclair, and I sink into it all. "You look good like that, Mac."

"Exhausted?" I ask, and he clenches his jaw.

"In my bed."

Well then . . . Nixon leaves his sweats on but yanks his tight tank over his head, then crawls in behind me and pulls me to him. "Sleep, Mac. I've got you."

I'm not sure why, but those words strike the biggest blow my painstakingly built walls have ever taken. "Nix . . ."

I'm not sure what I'm trying to say.

I can't do this.

I'm scared to death to truly let you in and accept that you mean something to me.

I want so much more from you than lessons. But how am I supposed to tell you that when that's it—the thing at the core of all this that scares me most?

Nixon

Mackenzie fell asleep within minutes.

She fits perfectly in my arms and my life, and I'm pretty fucking sure fighting this is fighting a losing battle. This tiny woman owns me and probably has since I was thirteen.

She whimpers in her sleep and reaches for me, tucking her arm around my waist and running the tips of her nails up and down my traps.

"Sleep, beautiful," I whisper against her hair and soak her in.

Her soft curves line up with all the hard planes of my body.

Tempting me to take what I want and refuse to ever let it go.

I've worked my ass off for everything I've ever gotten in my life, I can work for this—for her too. She's worth it.

"I don't know why you're so good to me, Nixon Sinclair," she whispers in the darkness as she presses her lips to my chest.

"Because you're mine, Mac. I think you always have been. And I'll always protect you and take care of you."

Soft eyes look up at me through long lashes.

So damn beautiful.

"I don't know how to be anybody's, Nix. But if there was anyone I'd ever want to try to be that for, it's you." She drags her hands down my chest, tracing each indent of my abs and scraping her nails along the waistband of my boxers before she wraps them around my cock and squeezes. A hot chill skirts down my spine.

I gather the length of her hair around my fist with slow deliberation as she pumps me. My blood thickens as my spine pulls tight. And fuck me, she's stunning like this. Sleepy and needy and so damn open for me, but tonight isn't a lesson. Tonight, I just want to make her feel good.

I tug her head back by her hair and suck her pouty bottom lip between mine as I roll her onto her back.

"A new lesson?" she whispers against my skin.

"No, baby."

"Did I do something wrong?" Confusion shines in her golden eyes.

"You're perfect." I press my lips to hers. "Tonight isn't about lessons. I want you to relax. Let me make you feel good."

Mackenzie whimpers as I lick my way into her mouth, then down her neck, paying special attention to that sweet spot on her shoulder that makes her squirm before moving down to worship her perfect nipples. I run my rough hand up the inside of her soft thigh and spread her legs, settling in and shoving down my sweats.

I lick up the length of her sex through the expensive lace panties she favors before pulling them from her body.

"Nixon," she breathes out on the sweetest sigh.

Her tart taste explodes in my mouth as she writhes beneath me.

"I need to make sure you're ready for me, baby. I don't want to hurt you."

Her body trembles as her breathing quickens.

"I fucking love seeing you like this, Mac," I growl against her drenched cunt and drag my finger around her clit—careful not to touch, just to tease—before I push inside her as her moans get louder.

She clamps her knees against my head and grinds against my face, taking what she wants while I suck her pretty little swollen clit into my mouth.

I pull back and look up at her, just before slapping her pussy and stuffing her full with my fingers.

She jolts—her entire body tightening and releasing as a silent scream falls from her pouty, perfect lips.

So fucking beautiful and all fucking mine.

I lick her through her orgasm until her trembling body relaxes beneath me, then her knees loosen, and her thighs fall back to the bed.

Cradled between her legs, I reach for the condoms in my nightstand until her quiet voice breaks the silence. "Have you been tested, Nixon?"

"Last month, before practice started." I don't move, unsure of what she's saying.

"Me too. Not last month, but before I left DC. I'm clean, and we both know I haven't been with anyone else in years . . ."

"I haven't been with anyone else since I was tested, baby. But we don't have to do this," I tell her, trying to wrap my head around the trust I think she's giving me.

"I been on the shot for years, Nix . . . I'm clean. You're clean. And I don't want anything between us. Please," she pleads, like I'll ever be able to deny her a thing.

I gently run my thumb over her cheek. "Are you sure, baby?"

Mackenzie pulls my face down to her and presses her lips to mine softly as she wraps her legs around my waist. "I need you, Nixon. Just you." She kisses me again. Harder and longer. "Nothing between us. Just us."

And just when I think I'm starting to get where she's coming from, she bites my bottom lip, then sucks it into her mouth. "Don't be gentle."

Kenzie

Chapter 20

A gust of wind cracks the shades against the windowsill as the feral look in Nixon's eyes darkens to something beyond sexy.

I'm not sure when it happened. Was it quickly or years in the making?

It doesn't even matter when. This man owns me.

My body, my orgasms, and I think he might just own my heart too.

I'm not sure how it happened or when it happened, but it happened, and it's scary as hell.

With a wicked grin on his firm, full lips he drags the thick head of his cock through my drenched sex, covering himself in my arousal. Sliding up and down. Pushing in the tiniest bit, then pulling right back out and smacking my clit until it throbs in time with my heart.

My blood thrums through my veins, flowing just under my skin, excitement and arousal and something else fighting for dominance.

"Nixon . . ." I beg, desperate to feel him inside me. My nails score his skin as they dig into his shoulders, and I try to pull us closer. "Please. I want more."

My next breath is stolen from my lungs when he rolls us over and grabs behind my knees. "Straddle me, baby. I want to watch you ride me." His hands grip my hips. "But don't go thinking you're fucking me, Mac. It doesn't matter what position we're in. Your orgasms are mine."

"God, yes they are." Excitement courses through me as my body clenches, and I lean down and kiss the edge of his lips. "I was responsible for my own for far too long, Nix, and I want you to make me come. Just you."

I moan as he bucks beneath me, hitting my clit again.

"Tell me, Mac. Did you get yourself off this week?"

I shake my head and wrap my hand around his erection. "I tried. But nothing lived up to the memory of you. You've ruined me," I whimper.

"That's it. Up on your knees, beautiful. I want you to slide down my cock nice and slow. Feel the stretch, Mac." We both suck in our breaths as I do what he said and notch the head of his dick against my soaked entrance.

I lean forward and brace my hands on his chest, loving the feel of him. Of his strength. His power. The way he focuses it all on me. My God . . . it's too much.

Pleasure and pain spark like a bright bolt of lightning in a dark night's sky as he stretches me until I feel like I might just tear in half.

I move achingly slow as I take him deeper, and my eyes close as I soak it all in.

Every delicious sensation.

"Eyes on me, beautiful."

My eyes fly open and lock on his baby blues. I get lost in the emotion there as I take him deeper. Until I've taken all he's got to give me. I rock my hips, wanting this to last but chasing the high I've been missing since the last time I was in his arms.

"Fuck, baby, you're doing so good." He jackknifes up and

wraps my legs around his waist so we're chest to chest. Nix's strong arms band around my waist, and he takes back all control.

"My good girl . . ." he whispers as his lips press against mine, and I melt, loving the way he controls me.

"Only yours," I murmur against his lips and let him shift my body however he wants, unable to do anything but give myself over to him completely.

"Tell me, baby," he whispers in my ear. "Tell me what you want. Tell me how it feels. Tell me you're mine."

Oh. God.

This isn't what I should want. I want a career, not a man. We were supposed to be no strings. Instead, they're wrapping around us in a million directions, and instead of running, I just want more.

"You, Nix. I want you," I whisper back, relieved to give life to the words.

"I didn't say stop talking, Mac," he demands, and there's that growly voice I love. He changes our angle just enough to hit a whole new spot, and I see stars.

"More of this. More of us. I want you closer," I gasp. "Deeper. I want to feel you every time I move for fucking days." I lean my forehead against his and inhale his breaths.

His strokes are slow and measured. Controlled. Just like Nixon.

One hand grips my chin with rough fingers and holds my face while he takes my lips. He licks into my mouth as he fucks me harder. Faster. Our bodies moving together in an intricate dance. Moving against one another to our own beautiful choreography until I don't know where I stop and he starts. I just feel him. *Everywhere*.

"So fucking good for me."

His praise is like a lit match being thrown into a pool of gasoline.

A fire rips over my already hypersensitive skin, leaving a blazing inferno in its wake. It's too much but won't ever be enough.

"That's my girl," he growls against the hollow of my throat as his hips pick up speed and grinds his cock inside me, creating the most decadent friction against my clit and hitting the most delicious spot inside, and I know without a doubt I'm not going to last much longer.

A whimper is ripped from my lips on a sexy cry that even I can recognize as a beautiful sound.

"Shh, baby. I've got you."

I nod, unable to form words. Lost in my lust. Chasing the high.

Nixon drags his mouth over my peaked nipple, sucking and biting and scraping his teeth over my skin until the edges of my vision darken, and I think I may pass out.

Overstimulated . . . Overwhelmed.

"Gonna need you to come for me, Mackenzie." The flames lick higher and higher with each desperate word.

Every thrust of his hips against mine.

Each stroke of his fingers and cock. His teeth and tongue.

The look in those baby blues I could get lost in for days. It's all there. The lust. The need. The want. It's all reflected back at me, right there.

He's giving it to me in his words. His actions.

He's giving me *him*.

And as I wonder whether I can take it . . . take him, he thrusts up and slams me down against him, and I shatter in his arms. A silent scream falling from my lips as my body shakes violently, uncontrollably. There's nothing soft or gentle about it. It's world-defining and body-draining, but Nixon doesn't stop. He fucks me through my first orgasm, his strokes never stopping. His voice and body and actions holding me tightly while he pounds into me, adding a finger to play with my clit, then gripping my ass and opening me to him so he can play with that too.

I jerk with a mix of fear, anticipation, and pure need.

Willing to try whatever he wants.

To take whatever he'll give me.

"Nix . . ."

"Shh, beautiful. Relax and trust me," He croons, and a flicker of a flame comes roaring back to life. My body already primed for more. How could I not be when Nixon plays me like I'm the most important game of his life. Only he could ever do this to me. For me . . .

I press my lips to his shoulder and bite down as he teases me. Circling the puckered hole while he pounds into me in the most delicious way. And when he finally pushes his finger inside me as he pulls me down over him, I scream out in pleasure and come violently while Nixon roars my fucking name as he pulses and empties inside me.

He lays me down, dragging his fingers though my sex, gathering our release and pushing it back inside me. It shouldn't be hot as fuck, but with Nixon, everything is.

And hours later, after we've showered and fallen back in bed and back into each other's arms, I trace his tattoo and whisper a truth that scares me more than any other. "You scare the shit out of me, Nixon."

He presses his lips to the crown of my head and holds me close.

He doesn't push for me. He waits and lets me find my words.

Words that hurt on a primal level.

"I don't want to let you in, Nix. I don't want to need you. I don't want to love you. Because if I do . . . That kind of loss—that's the kind that has the power to break a person, and I don't think I could survive that again."

"Your mom," he whispers against my skin, and I nod, unable to form words as tears burn the backs of my eyes.

"Baby steps, Mackenzie. You're here. That's a start. Give me baby steps, and I'll give you everything I have."

I don't look at him, because if I do, he'll no doubt be able to see it all on my face. Every single thought. Every emotion. Every truth. And I already feel flayed open. I don't think I could take that. Not yet. Maybe not ever.

"Sleep, Mac. I'll be here all night to keep your demons away."

And the thing is, if anybody ever could, it would be him.

*W*hen I wake up the next morning, the bed is empty. Nixon is gone, and so is Gordie. There's no mistaking that one because the English Bulldog puppy snores loud enough to drown out all of downtown Kroydon Hills.

Do they make CPAPs for dogs?

I get out of bed carefully, deliciously sore and throw on the Boston U shirt Nixon gave me last night and my discarded panties. Luckily, he didn't rip these to shreds like he did my others. His condo mirrors mine, but it's more lived-in. The bedroom furniture is minimalist and stylish, but it's done with care, unlike my lack-of-furniture motif. Grays and blacks bleed into the en suite bathroom, where I help myself to his toothbrush, then fix my hair.

Hey . . . if he can use mine, I can use his.

I laugh at that thought and pad down the hall in search of coffee and stop, cursing myself for not considering that Leo would be here.

The younger Sinclair brother stands in the kitchen, shirt-less and shoeless. A pair of jeans hangs from lean hips while he waits for the coffee pot to finish brewing with his arms crossed over his chest.

For a brief second, I think about tucking tail and darting back to the safety of Nixon's room. That only lasts as long as it takes for Leo to laugh though.

"Might as well wait with me, Kenz. Pretty sure I heard you two going at it all night. You sounded very *enthusiastic*. You've gotta need the caffeine more than I do."

I've known Leo since he was in fourth grade and would pick his nose and eat it.

Maybe that familiarity is why I do what I do next.

I pick up an apple, toss it in the air, and catch it with one hand. "Hey, Leo . . ."

He looks at me with a cocky grin.

"Catch." Only instead of tossing the apple gently at his hands, I nail him in the nuts as hard as I can throw. "Now you need coffee and an ice pack. Sit down and shut the fuck up."

Leo doubles over in pain, and I help myself to a pack of peas in their freezer and toss them to him too. They land on the floor with a thunk because he can't bring himself to straighten out just yet.

I guide him over to one of the kitchen chairs and push him down into it, then hand him the peas and laugh when he flinches.

"What the actual fuck, Kenzie?" he groans, and I don't bother hiding my smile.

I pick up the apple next and toss it up in the air again, like I'm going to juggle. "Now, Leo. I know your Momma didn't raise you to talk to women that way." I throw it up and watch it come down.

"And I'm pretty sure you'd gut a man if they talked to one of your sisters that way." Another toss up and another catch, while Leo groans and adjusts the ice pack. "I also know if I told your brother what you just said, you'd be walking out of here with, at the very least, a black eye. He might go easy on you because he's your brother. But your team captain . . . my brother—he wouldn't be so kind."

"I was just kidding, Kenz." If that's his apology, he's going to have to do so much better.

I toss the apple one more time and wait until the last possible second to catch it. "Four years all state softball pitcher in high school. Don't piss me off, Sinclair."

"I'm sorry," his voice cracks as he screeches, and I smile.

The front door creaks open, and Gordie comes barreling into the kitchen, followed by his very sexy owner.

I squat down and let Gordie jump all over me like he didn't spend half the night sleeping by my feet.

Nixon hangs up Gordie's leash and cups my face as he drops a kiss on my head, and my face flushes because I like the familiarity of it. I probably shouldn't, but I do.

"What the hell, man? What's with the peas? What did you do?" he asks Leo, and I giggle.

"Let's just say Leo was trying to catch an apple, and it didn't go his way. Right, Leo?" I wait to see if he's going to tell Nixon what really happened or if he's going to save his own ass. Because I might not know where Nixon and I are headed, but I know with absolute certainty, he'd kill his brother for talking to me like that.

Leo glares. "Yeah. Something like that."

The coffee pot beeps, and I stand back and watch the sexiest man I've ever known make me a cup of coffee. Everly's right. Coffee is a love language.

Nixon hands it to me, then cups my ass right in front of

Leo and leans into my ear. "I fucking love you out of my clothes, but I gotta say, Mac, seeing you *in* them is pretty fucking great too."

"Jesus Christ. Get a fucking room," Leo whines, and I pick up the apple from the table. "Fuck. I'm kidding."

Yeah . . . that's what I thought.

Kenzie

Chapter 21

It's in the eyes . . . Always in the eyes.

—Kenzie's Secret Thoughts

I'm the first person to admit how quickly life can change. That doesn't mean I like change. It just means I know how precious time is. Change is still a bitch I fight constantly.

Nixon and I have kept things between us what I like to think of as low key. We're not hiding anything, but his schedule has been full steam ahead since the start of the hockey season. Most weeks, he's gone two, three, and sometimes four nights for away games, and another night or two for home games. Add that to the time I spend at the hospital, and most of the week, we're like ships passing in the night. But if he's in Kroydon Hills on that night, we're in bed together. And I've never slept better.

It works for us.

Leo knows. But then Nixon's younger brother has toned down the teasing ever since the apple incident. We haven't gone out of our way to broadcast it with anyone else yet. Yet being the operative word.

We're not hiding anything, no one has asked, surprisingly enough. But in all fairness, everyone has had a ton on their own plates, leaving us this perfect little space in time to figure out what the hell we're doing without them all butting in.

It's been incredible. But it's also coming to an end.

Nixon has been asking me to come to a home game since the season started, but my schedule hasn't worked out so far. Well that streak is coming to an end. I'm off Friday night, and the Revolution are playing Nixon's younger brother Hendrix's team that night, and he asked me if I'd come. I can't really say no.

I don't know what I'm supposed to do.

I've worked so hard to get where I am and spent so much time thinking I'd never find anyone who understood how important my job is to me . . . But he gets it. Hell, he supports it.

You always said you didn't need a man, and I didn't want to need one either. But I don't think I ever really had a chance. Not with Nixon. It's like the universe was waiting until the perfect time to bring us together, then decided to smack us both upside the head and say, hey, stop what you're doing and pay attention. This is important.

I just don't know . . . I don't know how to do it. How to open myself up to the kind of pain I could be inviting in? I wish you were here to help me through this.

I wipe the leaves off Mom's headstone and sit back on my heels.

Sometimes I think coming here is weird. It's not like I even open my mouth to talk to her. But in my mind, I have this entire conversation with my mom. Almost like a diary entry without the notebook.

The crunch of leaves behind me has me spinning to find Juliette walking toward me. She's wearing knee-high black boots and a long black coat Mom would have loved. And when I look past her, I see Becket standing next to the

Mercedes Benz AMG, giving Jules her space to be with Mom.

"Fancy meeting you here," she says with a sad smile as she lays a beautiful bouquet of daisies down on top of the headstone. "Happy birthday, Liz," she whispers, then sits on the marble bench next to Mom's grave. "You okay, Kenz?"

I nod, a little choked up.

"I still miss her," I whisper through a quiet sob. "I miss her so much, Jules."

She pats the seat next to her, and I sit down and lean my head on her shoulder.

"Me too, kiddo. Me too. It's been almost fifteen years, and I can still hear her voice in my head, telling me what to do."

I wipe my eyes and try to control my breathing. "I can't hear her voice anymore, and I really wish I could. There's so much I want to ask her."

Jules runs her hand over my head, smoothing my hair down my back, a sob catching in her throat. "I know I'll never be your mom, Kenzie, but I hope you know I'll always be here for you, no matter what."

"Oh, Juliette. I know that. I promise you, I know. I've just been so stuck in my own head lately, and I keep remembering this one thing she used to say. I wish I could ask her about it." My heart feels like it's cracking in half. "I hope you know if I couldn't have my mom, you were always the next best thing, Jules. I can't imagine what I would have done without you in my life."

She pulls me into a hug and holds me there.

"You are the only daughter I will ever have, Mackenzie. It doesn't matter that I didn't give birth to you. You're still mine, and your mom was willing to share you with me if she had to . . ."

"Great," I say between tears. "Now we're both crying."

"Yeah . . . Liz and I used to do that a lot too. You look so much like her." She wipes her face, then reaches inside her Chanel purse. Always Chanel for Jules. She pulls out a folded piece of paper, frayed from years of opening and refolding, and runs a hand over it reverently. "I've kept this for nearly fifteen years. I used to read it whenever I wasn't sure what I was doing and I needed some Liz energy."

She hands the paper to me, then waits as I look at it, immediately recognizing the looping J of Mom's hand-writing in Juliette's name written across the top. I slowly peel it open, careful not to rip the decades old paper.

JULES,

IF YOU'RE READING THIS, THEN I GUESS I DID THE RIGHT THING IN WRITING IT.

SON OF A BITCH. I REALLY DIDN'T WANT YOU TO EVER HAVE TO SEE THIS. SOMETIMES I DESPISE MY NEED TO BE RESPONSIBLE AND ORGANIZED. BUT I THINK THOSE TWO QUALITIES MAY COME IN HANDY FOR YOU.

A FEW DAYS AGO, I HAD TO GO TO A FUNERAL AND ENDED UP CONSOLING A COWORKER WHOSE HUSBAND HAD DIED UNEXPECTEDLY. I JUST KEPT THINKING HOW LUCKY THEIR KIDS WERE TO STILL HAVE THEIR MOTHER. THAT LED ME DOWN A RABBIT HOLE. IF SOMETHING HAPPENED TO ME, WHO WOULD MY KIDS HAVE? MY MOM AND STEPDAD? THAT CAN'T HAPPEN. JESUS. I COULDN'T GET OUT OF THAT HOUSE FAST ENOUGH. THERE'S NO WAY I'D EVER WANT TO PUT MY BABIES THROUGH THAT KIND OF LOVELESS CHILDHOOD.

I'M A LITTLE EMBARRASSED TO SAY, UNTIL NOW,

I'VE NEVER DRAWN UP A WILL BEFORE. I'VE HAD LIFE INSURANCE, BUT THAT'S AS MUCH AS I'VE DONE. I'VE FIXED THAT. THERE'S A TRUST FOR THE KIDS, AND YOU'RE THE TRUSTEE. THERE SHOULD BE MORE THAN ENOUGH FOR ANYTHING YOU COULD NEED.

ONCE EVERYTHING WAS SET UP, I PICKED UP THE PHONE TO CALL YOU.

I SWEAR I DID. HELL, I'M STARING AT IT AGAIN AS I WRITE THIS.

BUT I GUESS I'M A CHICKEN SHIT, BECAUSE I STARED AT THE DAMN PHONE FOR SO LONG, I THOUGHT I WAS BEING SILLY AND PARANOID. NOTHING WAS ACTUALLY GOING TO HAPPEN TO ME. THIS IS JUST A PRECAUTION.

EVEN AS I SIT HERE WRITING THIS LETTER AND CRYING INTO MY RED WINE AT THE MERE THOUGHT OF NOT BEING HERE, I KNOW I'M BEING RIDICULOUS. I REALLY HOPE THE ONLY TIME YOU SEE THIS IS WHEN WE'RE OLD AND GRAY, SITTING NEXT TO EACH OTHER WITH SWEET TEAS SPIKED WITH GOOD VODKA AND LAUGHING AT HOW STUPID I WAS . . .

BUT JUST IN CASE I'M NOT, HERE GOES.

THE ONLY PERSON IN THIS WORLD I TRUST TO LOVE MY BABIES ANYWHERE NEAR AS MUCH AS I DO IS YOU, JULIETTE. I CAN ONLY IMAGINE IF YOU'RE READING THIS, SOMETHING HORRIBLE AND COMPLETELY UNEXPECTED HAS HAPPENED, AND IF I KNOW YOU, YOUR HEAD IS SPINNING. BUT HERE'S THE THING, JULES. I NEED YOU. EASTON AND KENZIE NEED YOU. YOU'VE ALWAYS BEEN SO GOOD AT JUMPING INTO LIFE FEET FIRST, AND I'M GOING TO NEED YOU TO DO THAT ONE MORE TIME FOR ME.

Take tonight and get your shit together, Jules. Figure out whatever you need to figure out, then go get my kids. I'm guessing my mom has them.

Go. Get. Them.

Do it before she fucks them up the way she fucks everything else up.

Love them, Juliette. The rest will come.

Love them enough for me and you.

Love them enough that me not being there doesn't destroy my beautiful babies.

Promise me you'll never let them forget how much I love them.

And try not to screw them up too much, okay?

I love you . . . Always.

Liz

I finish reading it, then read it two more times before I look back at Juliette.

Tears are streaming down both our faces.

She wipes mine first, then takes my hand in hers. "I've never shared that letter with another living soul. Not even Becket has read it."

"Really?" I ask as my chest shakes with the force it takes to hold back my sobs.

"But you and Becks don't hide things from each other." Even as kids, if one of them knew something, that meant they both knew. There was no hiding in our house growing up. It's just the kind of kick-ass relationship they have.

"One day . . . Not today, but one day, I'm going to tell you how your mother managed to give me Becket Kingston after she died when she gave me you and your brother. And how, in a way, that means I have her to thank for Blaise too. Losing your mom was the worst thing that ever happened to me." She lifts my chin to see my eyes. "I need you to understand what I'm about to say."

I nod silently.

"Out of that pain came the best things that ever happened to me too. I hope I loved you enough for her and me, sweetheart. I hope I loved you enough that her death didn't break you."

She throws her arms around me and squeezes as she cries, and I end up rubbing her back. "It's okay, Jules. You and Becks were everything I could have ever asked for. And her death didn't destroy me, but I can't lie and say it didn't fuck me up. I don't know how to stop worrying that the other shoe is going to drop. That the more I love, the more I have that I can lose."

It's the first time I've ever put a voice to my fears, and my God, it hurts.

"Oh, honey. Is this about you and Nixon?"

"You knew?" I ask, half laughing, half sobbing. "How?"

"The day Brynnie gave birth to Knight." She smiles and takes my hand in hers. "Becket talked to Nixon."

"Oh no . . ." My mind starts spinning. "Was it bad?"

"No, Kenz. It was good. That boy has grown into quite the impressive man, and Becket isn't easily impressed. We've been trying to give you space, but now, I'm wondering if that was the wrong move."

I lace my fingers with hers and shake my head. "No, it was the best thing you could have possibly done. I needed that. I . . . I'm struggling, Jules. I don't know how to have it all, and I wasn't even sure I wanted it all. But then I found Nixon. Not found him, found him. He wasn't lost. But he's not the

189

guy I remember from high school . . . He's so much more." I look off into the woods behind the cemetery and try to gather my thoughts so I can put them into words. "He's everything, Jules. Everything. Which means if he's taken away, I don't know what I'd do. I don't think I could go through that kind of devastation twice."

"Oh, Mackenzie. You can't live your life in fear. That's not living. Don't let your mother's death do that to you. She'd never want that for you. If you want to worry about balancing a life and a career, talk to me. Talk to your aunts. They're some of the strongest women I've ever known. Hell, talk to Nixon's mom. She lost her parents, had to raise her brother, and was nearly killed while she was pregnant with the twins. And I swear that woman is one of the few women I've ever met who rivals your aunt Scarlet's strength. Balancing it all isn't easy. But nothing worth having ever is."

"I feel like I've heard that before," I tell her softly as I try to gather my spiraling thoughts.

"Is he good to you? Because at the end of the day, that's all that matters. If a man loves you and is good to you, and you can be happy together . . . Listen to that again. You can be happy together, because no man or woman can make you happy. It's not their job. You have to be happy with yourself to be happy with them. Like I said, if you can be happy together, you can work out the rest. The schedules. The families. The babies. The rest falls into place if you're willing to work for it. And you, my darling girl, have never been scared of a little hard work."

She stands and pulls me to my feet, then wraps an arm around my shoulders and angles us toward the sun. "I'd dare say you thrive on hard work. And if ever there was a thing worth working hard for, it's love. And if Nixon is that person for you, I want you to remember something . . ."

She trails off as I hang on every word.

"The same way your mother gave me my life—my husband and my three kids because I like to think I have shared custody with Liz. That same way, she gave you Nixon. You may never have met him if you didn't come to Kroydon Hills."

I close my eyes and tilt my face toward the sun and try to wrap my head around everything Juliette just said.

If you can hear this, Mom.

Thank you.

I look up from the ice as we're all skating off at the end of practice to find Hunter talking with our assistant coach, Jace Kingston. Pretty sure he's Jace and Deacon's agent too. Ironically, Dad was one of his first clients back in the day. Now he represents all three of his sons.

Oh yeah, and he's pissed as hell. "Sinclair," he calls out, and Leo shoves me.

"You're the Sinclair in trouble this time, asshat," Leo throws my way as he skates off like a little bitch who wants to avoid guilt by association.

I skate over to the boards and wait for him to finish his talk with Jace.

Then he waits for Jace to walk away before turning his pissed-off glare my way.

You," he snaps. "Do you have any idea how big the wait-list is to be one of my clients? That's right, asshole. I said wait-list. Athletes are *waiting* for me to take them on. Begging for me to help them. And you, you little shitstain. You, who was still a sperm in your daddy's dick when I made my first million, can't be bothered to pick up the goddamned phone. What the actual fuck, Sinclair? If Declan wasn't one of my first fucking clients—and someone I consider an actual friend in a business where you don't make friends—I'd shitcan your fucking ass."

"I can't talk here, man," I tell him as I look around to see who's paying attention, and he whistles like he's awed.

"Holy fucking shit, ladies and gentlemen, he can speak."

"Hunt—"

"No. Shut the fuck up. Your time to speak was any time over the past few weeks. Now, you listen. You're going to get changed, and then you and me, we're going to drive to your house, and you're going to tell me where your fucking head's at, because it sure isn't attached to your goddamn shoulders right now, man."

"Leo will be at my place," I tell him, not sure I want my brother involved in this meeting but knowing this is on me.

"Not my fucking problem. I could be home in my bed, fucking my wife today. Have you seen my wife, Sinclair? She's incredible. Smart and sweet and so goddamned sexy. She's also off on Thursdays. And do you know what we do when she's off on Thursdays?"

Pretty sure answering that is career suicide.

We stare at each other, neither of us willing to budge until Hunter finally breaks.

"What the fuck are you waiting for? Fucking go. I don't have all goddamned day." He looks away with a cocky grin. "Fucking lucky I like you, kid."

"Doesn't hurt that you've made millions off me already either, Hunt." He's not the only cocky fuck standing here. He's just louder about it.

"Yeah, that doesn't hurt. Now go before I get really mad."

I wait for another minute, just to get under his skin, then head for the locker room.

*H*unter looks ridiculous sitting at my kitchen table in his fifteen-thousand-dollar Brioni suit. "What the fuck is your dog doing?"

"Who the fuck wears a fuzzy suit anyway? Gordie probably thinks you killed his brother and wrapped him around your legs," Leo asks him before he pets Gordie on the head and sits down across from Hunter.

"Someone who can buy and sell you without blinking an eye, Leo. And it's cashmere, not fucking fur. Now how about you run along and let the men talk."

"Why you gotta be like that, Hunt?" Leo asks, and I laugh before he points at me. "The walls are thin. Just ask your girlfriend. I'm going to hear everything you say anyway."

"You repeat a fucking word of it, and I'll tell Dad about the time you lost his Super Bowl ring and didn't tell him about it," I warn.

"I found it before he even realized it was missing," Leo tries to defend himself.

"You found it three months later. You're just fucking lucky he never gave a shit about those things. Now sit down. Shut up. And don't repeat a goddamn word. Got it?"

Leo mimes zipping his lips, and I'm not sure who looks more annoyed, Hunter or me.

"I think having him here is a bad idea. But it's your funeral, Nixon."

I shrug and wait, bracing for the blowback because there's no way this is going to go well.

"I put the word out you'd be open to a trade in the offseason, and quite a few teams were interested. Of those interested, three were willing to work within your salary specifications. One has a player I happen to know the Revolution would give their left nut for. Deacon has been trying to get him on the team since he came on as head coach, and it's never worked out." He pulls an envelope from his inside pocket and slides it across the table. My office sent this information via email, as well, but considering you won't fucking answer me, I have no idea whether you looked at it."

I take the envelope and fold it in half.

That email has been sitting unopened in my account for a few weeks.

So have the two that followed.

"Now it's my turn to ask a question. Why the fuck did you have me go to the trouble of doing all this—and doing it quietly, which meant pulling all sorts of favors to get it done —if you had no intention of taking a trade?"

"I never said I wasn't interested," I answer, and Leo's eyes bulge the fuck out of his head.

"Your actions say it, even if your voice is too fucking scared to say it, Sinclair." Hunter leans back in his chair, but not Leo.

Leo grips the edge of the table as he glares. "What the fuck, man? I thought you might be looking for a trade, but I figured I was wrong because you'd tell me something like that. Way to man the fuck up, Nix."

"Fuck you, Leo."

"I'm on Leo's side for once," Hunter adds, and Leo's head whips his way.

"For once? You're my fucking agent too."

Hunter shrugs. "Not here for you." He turns my way. "You, however, I'd like an answer from you."

"I don't have an answer for you right now. My reasons for wanting the trade are still valid, I just don't know that they're enough," I admit.

"What fucking reasons? Because you don't like being a

Sinclair?" Leo pushes, seriously pissed now. "News flash, brother. You're going to be a Sinclair in Atlanta and Chicago too."

Hunter fakes a ridiculous cough. "DC." Then the fuck coughs again for good measure.

"Fine. You think they've never heard of Dad or Grandpa in DC, dude? You're going to be a Sinclair no matter where you go."

I push off the wall I've been leaning against and smack the damn envelope against the table. "I never said I didn't want to be a Sinclair. I just wanted to consider being in a city that didn't worship them."

"That sounds past tense. Has something changed?" Hunter asks, sharp as ever.

"Yeah, he met a girl," Leo tells him.

"Well fuck. That explains it all," Hunter agrees and smiles.

Not all of it. But it makes a fucking difference.

KENZIE

Hey Nix. I'm on my way home from the office and was going to pick up takeout from West End. You want anything?

NIXON

You.

KENZIE

Good answer, Sinclair.

NIXON

I have a present for you.

KENZIE

An orgasm?

NIXON

I like the way you think, Hayes.

KENZIE

Tik tock, Sinclair. What do you want for dinner and should I get some for Leo?

NIXON

Fuck Leo. Let him get his own hot girlfriend.

KENZIE

Why do I feel like I'm trying to herd squirrels right now?

NIXON

Squirrels aren't big and masculine, baby. I mean, if you said bulls or lions, it would be a little sexier.

KENZIE

Did Leo steal your phone?

NIXON

Does Leo know how to give you multiple orgasms?

KENZIE

Hopefully not.

NIXON

Hopefully? WTF Kenzie? You're killing me.

KENZIE

Hey! Don't Kenzie me.

NIXON

Don't tease me about my brother and your orgasms.

KENZIE

You started it.

NIXON

I'll be finishing it too.

KENZIE

I'm counting on it. See you soon.

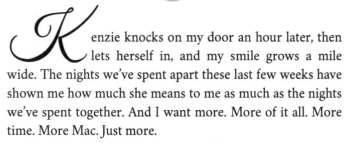

*K*enzie knocks on my door an hour later, then lets herself in, and my smile grows a mile wide. The nights we've spent apart these last few weeks have shown me how much she means to me as much as the nights we've spent together. And I want more. More of it all. More time. More Mac. Just more.

I fucking love this woman, even if she's not ready to hear it yet.

I cup the back of her head in my hand, and she lifts up on her toes and brushes her lips over mine, sighing. Her whole body relaxes the minute we touch, and my ego grows every single time that happens, knowing I did that for her.

She hands me a to-go box and smiles. "For Leo."

Like a heat-seeking missile, he walks out of his room at the first smell of food. "Did I hear *for me?*"

"Damn," she murmurs. "Either these walls really are paper thin or you have the hearing of a wax moth."

"What the fuck?" Leo asks as he takes the box and groans at the burger she got him. "What's a fucking wax moth, Kenz?"

"The animal with the best hearing in the world," she tells him like it's common knowledge. My girl is a fucking sexy little genius.

I wrap her arms around my neck and lift her off her feet, not willing to share what little time we get alone with my brother. "Watch Gordie for me, man."

"Bye Leo," she giggles, and goddamn, that smile. I'd go to war for that smile.

"What? No dessert?" he jokes.

With one hand around her ass, I grab the bag I left next to the door earlier and carry her down the hall to her place.

"Baby, your laughter is one of my favorite sounds in the world," I tell her as I set her down inside.

"Oh yeah?" She smiles as she sits on the couch and grabs a glass of wine from the table in front of it where she already has our dinner set up. "What's your favorite?"

"It comes in second to the sexy little way you moan my name when you come." I sit down next to her and press my lips behind her ear. "But it's a close second."

She smiles with her whole heart, and man, she's beautiful.

I take the bag I grabbed earlier and drop it in her lap.

"I didn't need a present, Nixon."

"Open it," I tell her, waiting to see her reaction, and she doesn't disappoint.

"Did you really get me a Sinclair Hoodie?" She giggles. "Why don't you just urinate on me and mark your territory, Nix?"

"Baby, if I thought you'd be into it, I wouldn't say no." I'm full of fucking shit and draw a big goddamn line at that, but Mac just shakes her head and dives back into the bag.

This time, she pulls out a matching v-neck t-shirt with my name and number on the back, which she adds to the pile before carefully pulling out the final piece. She opens the tissue paper like a kid on Christmas morning, then holds up my jersey. "Nixon . . . I love it."

Yeah, Mac . . . me too.

"I thought maybe you'd want to wear that tomorrow night at the game." This is new territory for us. We haven't exactly gone public yet, and that jersey would be about as public as it gets.

She folds the red jersey carefully on her lap, then runs a hand over it. "Are you asking or telling?"

"Asking, Mac. This one is up to you. But I know what I want." I've known what I've wanted for a while now. But I'm not putting added pressure on her. "Baby steps, right?"

"Uh-huh," she whispers and looks down at the jersey again. "You called me your girlfriend earlier. In that text . . . you said, Leo could get his own hot girlfriend."

"What can I say, baby? I told you I don't share. Not even with my brothers." I run my hand over her cheek, then cup her face. "Not you, Mac. Never you."

"If we do this, there's no going back," she whispers, like the words are so powerful, she needs to give them reverence. And I think I might fall a little bit more in love with her for it.

"I don't need an escape plan. I'm all-in, Mac. You and me." There's no fear or hesitation in my voice, and Mac snuggles into my hand.

"I'm scared, Nix." Her warm eyes lock on mine, and the fear shining back guts me. "I keep waiting for the other shoe to drop. My life has been really good for a long time, but not this good. I don't remember the last time I was as happy as I've been since I came home, and I'm scared to death that I'm tempting fate or something. What happens when that shoe drops?"

"What happens if it never drops, and you've spent your life waiting for it instead of living?" I remember something Dad said and smile as I brush my lips over hers. "Time's a thief, Mac. Don't give it any more than you have to give. Don't live your life in fear of the what-if."

"I don't know if I can do that, Nix." She climbs into my lap and presses her forehead to mine. "But for you, I'll try. Only for you," she tells me, echoing my earlier words. "Only ever you."

My inner caveman roars to life, possessive as fuck at finally hearing those words. Words I've been dying to fucking hear for weeks. "Does that make you my girlfriend?" I ask with my lips pressed to hers. "Because I've got to tell you, sixteen-year-old me, would have jizzed his pants if he knew one day Mackenzie Hayes would be his girlfriend."

"Oh yeah?" She kisses one corner of my mouth, then the other before she pulls her shirt over her head and tosses it to the floor. "What would sixteen-year-old Nixon have done if he knew he was about to get to touch my boobs?"

"He sure as hell wouldn't have had a clue what to do with them." I lick into her mouth, dinner long forgotten, and she pulls back just enough to look into my eyes.

"Guess it's a good thing I waited for you then, Sinclair."

Her words are like a balm to my tired soul, erasing the bone-deep exhaustion left over from my meeting with Hunter and the decision that had to be made.

"I love bossy Nixon." She shifts her hips, and a tiny moan slips past her lips.

"Good. Now get on your knees and show me."

My biggest flex in life is I already know my soulmate. All four of them, actually, and they've been my best friends for fifteen years. Ten out of ten, recommend.

—Kenzie's Secret Thoughts

*N*ixon presses his lips to my forehead, and I open my eyes. "You leaving?" I ask, still half asleep.

"Yeah, baby. Go back to sleep. I'll see you tonight." He kisses me again, and I pull him down to me and think about holding him here so I can hide from the world a little bit longer.

"I'm going to talk to your sisters this morning, so I don't blindside them tonight. Just letting you know."

"Have fun with that." He pulls back and pulls the blanket up to cover my naked chest. "You make it really hard to want to leave, Mac."

"Then don't," I murmur, still not ready to burst our bubble.

"Don't tempt me." He shakes his head and walks away, and I feel the loss on a molecular level and wonder when exactly that happened. When did hesitation turn to want and want turn to need? Actual physical need?

I don't have to be in the office until noon today, so I grab my phone from the nightstand and shoot off a text to the girls.

KENZIE

Anyone around for coffee this morning?

BRYNLEE

If you don't mind Knight attached to my boob because that's the only time he doesn't cry, I'm in. But seriously . . . do I have to shower?

GRACIE

Umm . . . That's a no-go for me. The smell of coffee makes me want to vomit.

EVERLY

Everything makes you want to vomit.

GRACIE

You're not wrong.

KENZIE

Didn't the medicine help?

GRACIE

Well I'm not actually vomiting anymore, but feeling like I'm going to is almost as bad. I swear to God, you're tying my tubes the second these babies are out of me. I'm not doing this again.

LINDY

You said that after the twins.

GRACIE

Yeah well, I didn't know the next time I'd be having triplets. Seriously, how the hell did this happen?

EVERLY

Maybe if you'd get off your husband's dick every now and then, you wouldn't always be knocked-up. Just saying.

BRYNLEE

Shots fired. Who pissed in your cheerios, Evie?

LINDY

She's just pissed because Cross went and got snipped, and they can't have sex for a week or two.

EVERLY

Listen, three kids are plenty. And unlike Gracie, I have no need to test my luck with twins or triplets. And holy shit, do those genes run strong in our family.

LINDY

We've got appointments booked all day today, Kenz. Rain check?

KENZIE

Okay – let me rephrase.

Anybody going to the Revolution game tonight?

LINDY

I am.

EVERLY

Me.

BRYNLEE

Not unless you want to see my jumbo boobs on the jumbotron.

LINDY

No. Just no. Put them away and get him a pacifier, Brynnie.

GRACIE

Doubtful at this rate, but maybe. I want to see Hendrix.

Good grief, they don't make it easy.

KENZIE

Well I'll be there, and I'm probably going to be wearing Nixon's jersey.

EVERLY

Still doing the fake-a-date thing?

LINDY

Report the motherfucker to HR and move on. No one should have this much power over you, Kenzie. Dr. Dick has got to go if this is legitimately the only way you can deal with him.

KENZIE

Not a fake-a-date.

EVERLY

I'm lost. Huh?

BRYNLEE

OMG. Follow the breadcrumbs people. She's been boinking your brother's brains out for weeks, guys. How has nobody noticed? I have a newborn and I knew.

GRACIE

I'm sorry. What!?

EVERLY

Brynnie knew!

LINDY

Your brother is going to shit.

KENZIE

You are not going to tell my brother today. Do not fuck this game up for them, Lindy, or I will . . . Fuck. I don't know what I'll do. But don't say anything. I'll talk to Easton tomorrow.

LINDY

The hell you will. If you want Nixon to live long enough to one day give you multiple orgasms, that man is going to have to talk to your extremely overprotective brother himself.

KENZIE

. . .

GRACIE

Kenzie???

KENZIE

Well . . . umm, technically, he's already lived through the multiple orgasms many, many, MANY times. What can I say? He's an overachiever. Ohh, and he's really bossy too.

EVERLY

You dirty dog. You really have been boinking his brains out.

GRACIE

I might throw up.

EVERLY

Everything makes you throw up.

GRACIE

Not like this. You're really boinking Nixon?

KENZIE

We're grown women. Can we please stop saying boinking?

BRYNLEE

Is the sex good?

LINDY

Multiple orgasms, Brynnie. Did you miss that???

KENZIE

So fucking good. I never knew it could be like this. Like seriously, I had no clue I'd love sucking dick as much as I do. I mean . . . you guys always said it was fun, but I didn't believe you. Now I get it.

EVERLY

Eww. That's my brother.

LINDY

Yup. And your brother likes pussy, sweetie. Time to build a bridge and get over it.

GRACIE

Ohh, you're a mean little twat waffle, aren't you?

LINDY

Twat waffle?

GRACIE

Leave me alone. It's the best I could come up with. Seriously . . . You're sleeping with Nixon?

KENZIE

It's more than that, guys. He's not just a giant sex toy to play with.

LINDY

But he is a giant, isn't he? You waited forever for good dick. I really hope it's big and curves just enough.

GRACIE

Yup. I just threw up. Thanks for that.

KENZIE

I mean, clinically speaking . . . yeah. Fuck it. Even by textbook examples, he's pretty fucking big.

GRACIE

Please stop. I'm begging. I haven't eaten enough to puke any more than I already have.

BRYNLEE

Guys. The way he was looking at her when she was holding Knight. Our boy is gone for our girl.

LINDY

Could you make us sound any more incestuous!

GRACIE

Wait. Is it really more than sex?

EVERLY

Okay. Serious talk for a minute here. I can't believe you even have to ask that. I didn't see him watching her holding Knight, but I know the look. It's the one Nixon's had on his face since the first time you slept over and wore a bikini. Pretty sure he jerked off to that image all through high school.

BRYNLEE

Umm, eww. Leave it to you to ruin what started as such a promising statement.

LINDY

It's a compliment.

GRACIE

Umm . . .

KENZIE

He did not.

GRACIE

Shut up. Even you couldn't have been that oblivious, Kenzie.

KENZIE

Even me? What does that mean?

LINDY

It means you never realized the way everyone looked at you because you didn't care. You had us, and you had sports and books, and you never really cared about boys. Not back then. And those high school boys were looking. You were, and still are, hot as hell. And what's hotter is that you don't even know it. You really were oblivious.

BRYNLEE

Gonna go out on a limb here and say you had her until you said oblivious again.

KENZIE

Yeah, not loving that word.

EVERLY

You're smart. And hot. And a goddamned doctor. You need a flaw, Kenz. Be grateful oblivious is the worst of it and you don't have ugly feet or something.

BRYNLEE

Ugly feet?

EVERLY

It was the best I could come up with. I can't tease her about the sex. It's Nixon, and even I have lines I can't cross. At least not yet. Give me time to work on it, and I'm sure I'll get past that little hang-up.

GRACIE

Not me. I don't want to hear about my brother's junk.

KENZIE

Better get used to it. You've all tortured me about Easton and Lindy for years. Payback's a bitch.

LINDY

Let's see. Do you prefer to suck his dick on your knees or on the bed because Easton likes it when I'm on my knees and he can tug my hair.

KENZIE

What the fuck!

LINDY

Just saying. There are ways I can control three out of four of you now. This is going to be fun.

BRYNLEE

You know you're a little scary, right?

LINDY

Yup. See you all tonight.

GRACIE

I didn't say I was going.

LINDY

Oh sweeties. You're not going to want to miss these fireworks.

KENZIE

Do. Not. Tell. My. Brother.

LINDY

One hundred bucks and the right to talk about your brother's cock whenever I want says I won't have to tell him.

KENZIE

Just had to bring the cock up one more time, didn't you?

LINDY

Yup. Game on.

SCOOP OF THE CENTURY

Hello, all you beautiful people.

An apology is in order. It's official. I was outscooped. And we all know how much I hate to be outscooped. According to footage just shared to this reporter's tipline, it looks like one of our favorite Kroydon Hills socialites was just spotted walking into the Revolution Arena with a certain name and number on her back that doesn't belong to her big brother. Is one of our favorite puck packers dating his team captain's little sister?

Looks like I have a new mission to fulfill, and I won't rest until it's been completed and I can confirm or deny. Check back soon for all the dirty deets.

#KroydonKronicles #ScoopOfTheCentury
#PuckPackPlusOne

Nixon

Chapter 24

The music blasts through the speaker as the arena comes to life around us. Excitement and energy doing their job to help pump us up while we warm up as a team. I'm stretching out my quads when a pair of skates stops in front of me, and I hear a teammate yell to *get back on your own side of the ice.*

I look up and see my little brother come to a stop in front of me. He smirks around his mouth guard. "You look kinda out of shape, brother."

I stand and shove Hendrix away with a laugh. "Yeah well, you still skate slow as shit. No clue how the fuck you made it to the NHL with those moves."

Leo skates over, and I hear a reporter yelling, "Nixon, Leo, Hendrix. Turn around and give us a shot."

Hendrix stands between us and throws an arm around each of our shoulders. "Get a good look now, because neither of these guys'll be smiling when I kick their asses and they lose tonight."

"Okay, big mouth." Cross, our actual team captain to Easton's co-captain, cuts his youngest brother-in-law off before he starts shit before the game. "No getting us all thrown in the sin bin before the puck's even been dropped."

"Wouldn't be the first Sinclair to do it," Hendrix points out and smiles.

"That shit was fun. I have no regrets," I tell them as Ares ices us all when he stops next to us.

"Are we having a tea party no one invited me to?" he asks with a dead serious look on his face.

"Just saying hi before all you fuckers are crying in your beer that you lost," Hendrix jokes. Fucker probably thinks that's actually happening, but he's got no clue. Our cold streak lasted exactly one week. As soon as we worked out the kinks and brought up a new winger from the farm team, things started clicking again. "Hey, there's the girls."

We all look over to where Hendrix is pointing at Gracie, Everly, Lindy, and Mackenzie.

"Oh, damn," Ares barks out as Easton skates over to the boards to say hi to Lindy and the kids.

"Somebody wanna tell me why Kenzie *Hayes* is wearing Nixon's jersey?"

"You didn't," Cross groans and shakes his head.

Leo laughs and looks at me. "Want me to protect you?"

"You can all fuck right off." I ignore whatever else they're saying as the most satisfying, possessive feeling I've had burns behind my ribs. Seeing this beautiful girl in my jersey, with my name stretched across the back, declaring her mine for the entire world to see . . . Yeah. That feeling isn't going away any time soon.

I skate over to where Mac stands behind the half-wall and pull off my helmet. "Hey, baby."

Her cheeks flame red as Everly fans herself, and fake whispers, "He called her *baby*."

"I'm going to be sick," Gracie groans, and she might be serious because she's a little green. But she's got a husband somewhere to worry about her, so for once, I'm worrying about my woman and me.

Like a goddamn magnet, I lean in, drawn to Mac, and claim her lips, dying to do more but knowing I can't. Not here. Not yet. "You came."

She smiles and tugs at the jersey. "I had some new clothes I wanted to wear. What do you think? It's not my last name, but it's not too shabby, right?" She teases me, and my blood roars in my ears.

Not her last name . . . yeah. We can change that.

The buzzer rings, signaling the end of warm-up. "You look fucking hot, baby. I want you in this and absolutely nothing else when I get home tonight."

Her beautiful face softens, and she touches my cheek. "Pretty sure I can make that happen. Now go win me a game, Sinclair."

I watch her walk away with the girls and stare until Easton pushes me ahead of him. "We're gonna fucking talk about this tomorrow."

"Whatever you say, man." I skate away, knowing I got the girl. Now I gotta win the game. Shouldn't be too hard.

*T*urns out, it wasn't that hard.

Chicago has been turning over the puck all night. Easy pickings. Like right now. Their center just cleared the puck, and the dumb fuck is taking it right up the middle.

Like I said. Easy pickings.

Cross slams into him, and the puck goes wide.

Ares takes control and passes to Leo. Leo dodges Hendrix and crosses it to me.

Yeah . . . Sorry, baby brother.

I circle the net, looking for my shot. And, *oh yeah*. There it is.

Upper right-hand corner. Fucking beautiful.

My team swarms, congratulating me on the goal and celebrating the lead that just closed out the game, 4–2. The Revolution wins. The stands are going wild as everyone tosses hats onto the ice. I look up into the stands, searching for the box Mac is watching in, and there she fucking is—my girl, in my jersey, with my family, screaming her lungs out.

Mine.

Fuck the rest of the world.

Fuck what they think or expect.

This is it.

This is what I want.

Her. This team. This town. This family. But it all starts and stops with her, and it's about time she hears it.

We line up to shake the other team's hand, and I take an extra second to smack Hendrix's helmet. "Good game, little brother."

"Nice hat trick, Nix. You showing off for your girl?"

"You're fucking right I am. You flying home tonight?"

Cross smacks the top of Hen's helmet too, then ushers me along. "Let's go, Sinclair."

"Go," Hendrix says. "We're flying out tonight. I'll see you at Christmas."

"See ya, Hen," I tell him before turning to leave.

"Hey, Nix," he calls out. "You're girl's a fucking smoke show. You outkicked your coverage, man." He skates off before I can kick his ass, and I laugh. Always the little shit-stirrer. Not wrong though. Mackenzie Hayes is out of my league.

She's her own league.

"Thought it was fake," Easton growls again as we skate off the ice together.

"I'm not doing this here, man," I tell him, not willing to have this fight tonight.

Tonight, I want to go home and show my girl how much it meant to have her here and why it's better to live in the moment than in fear of the other shoe dropping.

KENZIE

Hey. I left with Gracie and Everly. Gracie wasn't feeling good.

That was a great game, Nix. You were so fucking hot.

If a hat trick is when you score three times, what do they call it when you score four times? Because you're absolutely scoring tonight.

Come over when you get home. I'll leave the door unlocked for you.

And don't yell at me. I'll grab Gordie from your place. He can be my guard dog.

Maybe he could snore the would-be intruder to death.

When you said nothing but your jersey? Did you mean no panties?

I fucking love this girl.

I rush through showering and the post-game interviews as much as I can.

It's easy to ignore the ribbing from the guys in the locker room. Easton keeps his distance, but he's going to have to get the hell over whatever his problem is with Mac and me. I'll talk to him about it tomorrow.

The questions from reporters and paparazzi didn't catch me completely off guard. Apparently, we're high-profile. They all seem to be running with the whole *team captain's little sister* line, based on what they were asking.

I really don't care what they say. I just want to get home to Mac.

When Coach pulls me into his office as I'm walking out, I'm a little surprised. "Everything okay, Coach?"

"That's what I wanted to ask you, Nix." He sits down behind his desk, and I start to sweat what he might be talking about.

"Not sure what you're talking about. I'm good. That was a hell of a game," I assure him, wondering if he got word of the trade talk.

"It was. Nice hat trick. Listen, I know we have a relationship outside this office, but when we're inside this building, I'm your coach. And as your coach, I've got to say this. Keep your personal shit out of this locker room and off my ice. Got it?"

Oh. That.

"Got it," I snap, irritated at the idea that Easton's gonna be so pissed that Coach feels the need to preemptively address it.

"Listen, I'm not trying to be a dick, I just don't want your personal life to affect our season," he explains, and now I get pissed. What the fuck?

"Coach, are you telling me not to see Mackenzie Hayes?" I ask, really hoping I'm reading this whole fucking thing wrong.

"And if I was, would you stop?" Coach volleys back at me.

"Fuck no," I tell him without hesitation. "Not a chance."

"Good answer, Nix. Kenzie deserves that. That's what I think as your friend and hers. As your coach, I'm warning you, do not let this shit go sideways with my goddamn goalie. Got it?" He stands and waits for me to do the same.

"Yeah, Coach. I got it." I rise from the chair and shake his hand, knowing Easton's going to give me shit.

Guess I'm going to have to meet him before practice tomorrow to get this out of the way somewhere other than the locker room.

"Good. Now get the fuck out of here before my wife calls me and asks me how you guys looked together. Do you have any clue how much the girls talk? It's crazy. They're like a hive mind. If one of them knows something, they all do. How the hell did you manage to keep this thing under wraps for so long?"

I shrug. "You've gotta ask Mac. It's what she wanted, so it's what I did."

Coach shakes his head. "Get out of here before the paparazzi storm the gates, trying to get another picture. You know the one of the two of you before the game has already gone viral. Bryn sent me a TikTok of those romance book girls already using it in a video. It's gotten a million views since pregame."

"Thanks, Coach."

"Rest tonight, Sinclair. We're on a plane tomorrow for Ontario," he adds, clearly dismissing me.

Thirty minutes later, I'm pulling into our parking garage.

It seems like everyone else wants to know how I feel about Mackenzie Hayes.

It's about time she knows.

Kenzie

Chapter 25

In a world full of twat waffles, be French toast.

—Kenzie's Secret Thoughts

I look around my living room and wonder if it's too much.

A fire burns in the gas fireplace, and white pillar candles flicker around the mantle while I sing along to my favorite sexy playlist. And when I catch my reflection in the mirror, I almost don't recognize myself.

My cheeks are flushed, and my eyes are shining.

This woman is happy, not just content.

She's living, not just going through the motions, surviving.

There's a difference, and it's scary as hell.

But Nixon is worth being scared for. He's worth jumping in feet first because I know he'll be there to catch me. If Mom and Jules could do it, so can I.

I set a bowl of food and water in the kitchen for Gordie when I hear my door open and hope like crazy it's Nixon and not Callen or Maddox. I peek my head out, suddenly worried, but my fears vanish as soon as I see him.

Nixon Sinclair makes gray sweat pants look absolutely pornographic, and I'm here for it. "Hey, baby."

Yeah. I'm here for that voice and those words too. Not just here for them, hungry for them. For him. I walk silently across the room and run my hands under his shirt and up his rib cage. "Hi."

He takes my face in his hands, and the way he looks at me has me melting into a puddle of goo at his feet. It's reverent, and my heart threatens to beat right out of my chest.

"You okay, Nix?" I flatten my palms and press my entire body against his.

His thumb caresses my cheek, and he shakes his head. "I love you, Mackenzie Hayes. I'm not sure when it happened. I don't know if it was last week or last month, or if it was the first time you walked into my house when we were kids. But it happened, and it's real. Fuck. It's the most real thing in my life. You. You're it for me. You're everything. I'm not sure if you're ready to hear it—"

I silence him with a finger pressed gently against his lips, completely overcome with emotion. "I have no idea what I did to deserve you, Nixon. But somehow, you're still here, standing in front of me. You never rushed me. Never made me feel like I wasn't enough. You've given me the space I needed to come to it all on my own, and I'm there, Nix."

I look up at him.

Up at his handsome face and kind eyes.

That deliciously filthy mouth I love.

That I *love*.

I love him, and my God, it's everything.

"It might have taken me a little longer to get here, Nix. But I never do anything fast. I'm an overthinker. I need to look at something from every possible angle. I need to study it before I can jump in. And even then, I don't always jump. But with you . . ." I ghost my lips over his and dig my fingers into his hair. "With you, I want to jump. You're going to have to be patient with me though. I'm still going to be waiting for the other shoe to drop. But loving you, Nix . . . loving you is worth the fear."

He lifts me off my feet and carries me across the room, then drops down into my oversized chair. His big jersey barely covers my white-ruffle, panty-covered ass, and my matching white knee socks slide down under my knees, but the look in his heavy eyes says it all. "Fucking beautiful, baby. You should wear my name every day."

"Pretty sure they'd frown on that in the operating room, Sinclair." He anchors his hand in my hair at the nape of my neck possessively, and I swear I could stay just like this forever.

Nixon's eyes trace over my face like a warm caress, healing all the rough and tattered edges of my soul. "I'm going to need you to jump again, Mac. Take my hand and jump with me."

"Nixon . . ." I practically purr as he massages my neck. "I can try," I promise him quietly, scared to pop this bubble and shatter this moment we're lost in.

"Marry me, Mackenzie," he breathes against my lips so softly I'm not sure I heard him right.

"Nix—"

"Don't say no, Mac. Say *not yet* if you need to. I'll wait forever for you. But it's you and me, Mac, and I need you to know that. I don't care if you marry me today, tomorrow, or next year. But you're going to marry me because you're mine and I'm yours. I will never be anything but yours." He presses his lips against mine, swallowing my breath and stealing my soul.

We stay like that, just kissing, for what feels like hours.

But there's no *just* about kissing Nixon. It's so much more.

He's so much more.

"I love you," I whisper into the charged air enveloping us. "Only you. Only ever you."

His hand coasts down my back and under his jersey, stopping on the ruffled panties with a grin. "Did you buy these for me, Mac?"

His finger slips under the edge, and his eyes morph into two pools of melted steel.

Smoldering and sexy and dangerous to my heart.

"I did," I tell him as I raise up and tug his shirt over his head, then shove his sweats down enough to see my man is going commando. "Did you not wear anything for me?"

That sexy grin grows as he nods.

"Words, Sinclair," I echo back to him, giving him the words he loves to give me. I kiss his lips. His cheek. The hollow of his throat. "I need to hear your words."

Nixon slides my panties aside, and I guide him to my entrance.

"You want my words, baby?" he growls hot and powerfully, and my pussy clenches in response, desperate and needy and dying for him.

I slide down, taking him inside my body, and we both moan together at the utter perfection of the moment. At the feel. At us.

Nixon's hands go to my hips, and he leans back in my chair, then watches me as I rock slowly against him.

"How's this? Yeah, I went commando for you." He shifts and hits that spot that makes me see stars instantly.

"I bought this jersey because I wanted to see you in my name." His grip tightens on my hips, and I moan. "I wanted everyone to see my name on you, Mac. Everyone. Because I'm a greedy, selfish bastard who doesn't share and doesn't want any other poor fuck to think he even stands a chance."

"Nix . . ." I leverage my palms on his shoulders and circle my hips, loving the friction on my clit as much as the way he hits my G-spot with every snap of his powerful hips against mine. "Everything I've done for months has been for you. *You*. You're all I think about. All I want to think about. It's you, baby. Just you."

"Oh God." It's all too much.

His words.

His actions.

His love.

He leaves no room for doubt.

"Promise me, Nix," I pant and slowly squeeze him inside my body, loving the look of near devastation on his handsome face. "Promise you'll catch me when I fall."

"I'm going to be carrying you the whole way, Mac." His eyes glaze over, and I'm lost.

I'm his.

I always will be.

Nixon leans back so he can watch me the way he likes to and runs his deliciously rough hands up my body until he cups my breast and pinches my nipples, knowing exactly what he needs to do to get me there.

I come on a beautiful moan, my pussy throbbing around Nixon as he follows me over the cliff, and my name leaves his lips like a hallowed prayer only he'll ever say.

I drop my forehead to his and breathe in his breath. Needing to be closer.

"Yes," I whisper softly against his lips.

He lifts his head and looks at me with a new awe in his eyes. "Yes?"

"Really?" My normally crazy-confident man says, sounding a little shocked.

"Yeah, Nix. Really. I think it was always supposed to be us. It just needed to be our time. And we might have had a little push from my mom, but I don't want to cry right now, so I'll tell you about that later, okay?" My words are soft and sacred.

"It will only ever be us, baby."

"I love you, Nixon Sinclair," I tell him as I lay my head against his chest.

"I can't fucking wait for you to be my wife, Mac." He runs his hand over my hair, and I practically purr with contentment. "You gonna be Dr. Sinclair, baby?"

"Nope. I worked my ass off to be Dr. Hayes, Nix. I'm not giving that up. But I'll consider Dr. Hayes-Sinclair." I kiss above his heart, loving the sound of that.

"As long as you call yourself mine, you can call yourself whatever else you want, Mac. But you only wear my name from now on." His hand runs over my ruffles again. "And maybe these panties."

"Guess it's a good thing there's so many Sinclair jerseys to choose from," I tease, and he spanks my ass.

"My name. My number, baby. Unless we're at a football game. Then I might make an exception, but you better be wearing a big fat diamond ring by then." Fuck, I love possessive Nix.

"If I say no, will you spank me again?" I tease, ready for this man again.

"Where do you want to be spanked?" he asks, his voice deepening.

"How about we go to bed, and I'll tell you."

He rises with me in his arms and licks into my mouth.

Fuck, I love this man.

226

"Nix," I call into the bathroom where I left him in the shower. One of us has to get to work. "Your phone is ringing."

Where the heck is my other shoe?

I hate rushing around. I like to be early for things. For everything, really. But waking up in Nixon's arms makes it incredibly hard to want to get out of bed and get the day started. I'm okay with starting things, but they mainly involve the bed . . . and the shower.

Note to self—showering together does not save time.

That's a myth.

A fun myth to test out . . . one that involves multiple orgasms because my man believes in going big or going home. But a myth, nonetheless.

I squat down to see if maybe Gordie took my seven-hundred-and-fifty-dollar, purple tweed Manolo Blahnik and decided to make it his personal bitch of a chew toy under the bed. Wouldn't be the first shoe I'd lost to him. Probably won't be the last.

Shit.

I knock Nixon's phone off the bed when I pull the blanket off the floor.

"Nix . . . It looks like Hunter left you a text." I recognize his agent's name. He's Easton's agent too. Only as I set the phone on the nightstand in order to continue my hunt for my missing shoe, I see the text preview on Nix's phone's lock screen.

HUNTER

I need to know today if you're taking the trade. You asked for this. Now you need to deal with it. Take the trade, man. It's a lot of money.

My world tilts on its axis, and I slide my ass down to the floor as Gordie trots in with my shoe in his mouth and drops it in my lap.

Nixon walks in and looks from Gordie to me, then curses. "I'm sorry, baby. Did he eat another shoe?"

I look down at the expensive heel that's strangely unharmed and silently shake my head.

Nixon squats in front of me, concerned. "You okay, Mac? You're white as a ghost."

"I guess it only took a day." I run my hand along his cheek, then shove him back on his ass and stand up. I think about throwing my shoe at him but don't want to risk accidentally hitting Gordie.

"What the hell, Mac?" He doesn't move, just sits there, stunned.

Yeah, me too, I want to yell.

"I thought the universe brought us together. Serendipity, right? I mean, how many people find the love of their life in middle school at their best friends' house? But fate wasn't bringing us together. Nope. It was tempting me to take a chance so it could smack me back down and remind me what a cruel bitch it is." I level Nixon with an icy glare as he stands and reaches for me.

"Don't touch me," I warn him.

"What the hell are you talking about, Mac? I'm not following here. Help me out."

My anger grows like a wildfire catching on the Santa Ana

winds, and I throw his phone at his face. Nixon's reaction time is better than Leo's, and he catches it before it can crash into his nose.

"When were you going to tell me about the trade, Nixon?" I don't realize I'm yelling until it's too late, but I'm so worked up, there's no stopping it now. "You promised you'd catch me. You asked me to marry you."

I start pacing with one shoe on my foot and the other in my hand, my mind racing. Anger and heartbreak and disappointment all warring with each other.

"Oh my God. I said yes, and you *still* didn't think you needed to tell me you're leaving." My raised voice scares Gordie enough that he runs under the bed. "What is wrong with you?" I look around the room, searching for an answer I'm not going to get. "What the hell is wrong with me? How . . . how could you do this? I trusted you."

This time I do chuck my heel, but I aim for his foot.

"You fucking dick. I love you so much I don't want to hurt you, even though I want to kill you. Look at me."

"Baby . . ." he takes a step forward, and I move away.

"Don't you fucking *baby* me." I wipe my eyes, refusing to let any tears fall.

"Mackenzie. Shut up and listen to me."

My back snaps straight, and I think rage might be a visible thing because I'm seeing it in front of my eyes. If I could reach my shoe, I'd throw it harder this time and aim for a softer spot. Like his face.

"I asked about a possible trade before you even came home from DC." He takes a step forward and waits to see how I'm going to react. I am wearing another shoe, after all.

"I asked about it. I never said I'd take one. I wanted to know if it was possible. I *wanted* to know if putting a little space between myself and the Sinclair name in this town . . . the legacy that's expected. That needs to be lived up to. I thought some space could be a good thing. If it would help me figure out my own shit." He takes another step forward and reaches out his arms for me, but I don't move.

"I asked before you, Mac. And when Hunter flew in the other day to discuss options, I knew there was no option. I was staying here because *you* are my fucking home. If you're here, I'm here. When I told Hunter I wasn't interested, he refused to take my answer. He said to think about it and give him my answer today."

My shoulders relax a fraction of an inch, and when he takes the final step toward me, I don't back up. I don't touch him or let him touch me, but I don't move away. Not exactly relieved, but at least with a better understanding of where he's coming from.

"Once you came back into my life, I knew I couldn't take it, Mac."

I shake my head and shove him away. "How could you ask me to marry you and not tell me, Nixon? I'm not a little girl waiting to be told what to do. I might like bossy in the bedroom, but everywhere else, I'm strong enough to handle myself."

"You won't even tell Dr. Dick to back the fuck off or report him to HR, Mac."

My head snaps back like I've been physically slapped.

"Fuck you, Nix," I yell at him as my heart breaks inside my chest.

"You don't like confrontation," he backpedals. "And let's not forget that neither of us have been in a relationship before. You're not the only one who doesn't know what the fuck they're doing, baby. I'm sorry I didn't tell you, but I didn't think it mattered since I turned it down."

I shake my head and move around him toward the door and pick up my discarded shoe. "An apology should never contain the word *but*, Nixon."

"Where are you going?" he asks, and I stop in my tracks and look over my shoulder.

"I have to go to work," I snap at him, then slide on my shoe and walk into the other room, looking for my bag and keys.

"This isn't over, Mac," he insists, and he's not wrong. "We're not over."

It takes every ounce of strength I have to turn slowly to face him and keep my calm while I do it. "No. It's not over. But I have to go to work, and you have a flight to catch in a few hours."

"I'm sorry, Mac." He moves in behind me and wraps his arms around me. "I love you."

I close my eyes, completely overwhelmed. "I love you too, but I'm still furious with you. We can't keep things like this from each other if this is ever going to work."

He rests his chin on my shoulder, refusing to let go. "Does this mean you're not leaving me?"

"It means I'm pissed as hell. And I'm not sure how long it's going to take to get over it. But I have abandonment issues, Nix. I'll never just walk away. Now let me go, so I can be fucking pissed all day at work and you can get on the damn plane."

"I'm sorry, Mac. No *buts*. I'm an idiot."

"Yes, you are." I turn to look at him, still so fucking mad. "Have a safe flight and a good two games."

He moves in to kiss me, and I back out of his hold. "I've got to go."

"I love you, Mac,"

"I know," is all I'm able to say before I leave.

Damn it.

TRIPLE DECKER SANDWICH

Well damn, Kroydon Hills. I've never wanted to be the meat in a triple decker sandwich before, but it's official. You can call me bacon and slap me between three slices of bread, because seeing all three Sinclair brothers together on the ice last night has this reporter rethinking her stance on *the more the merrier*. Because those three men look like they could make a girl very *merry*.

If the video currently circulating on social media is to be believed, which I happen to think it is, the oldest of the Sinclairs' very own puck pack could be off the market.

It's a shame, if you ask me. I'm not sure a single woman could ever turn that man down again after practically impregnating the entire female population with one single kiss. Sorry, ladies. He's taken. But he does have two brothers.

#KroydonKronicles #PuckPack
#TripleDeckerSinclairSandwich

I park outside of Lindy and Easton's house and look at my text messages.

NIXON

I'm sorry I hurt you.

She left me on read.

Fuck.

I look up at the house in front of me and realize Easton is sitting on the porch with Lindy. Are they . . . *shit.* They're having coffee and staring at me.

Guess I'm about to ruin both Hayes siblings' mornings.

Lindy gets up and kisses my cheek. "Try not to die. I'd be a terrible prison wife." She turns to her husband and cups his cheek. "And you . . . Try to remember that you love your sister, and she's happy. And if you're going to fight him, do not fuck up my hydrangeas. They look pretty."

I laugh when she disappears inside, leaving me here with

Easton, who looks like he might actually consider killing me if he thought he could get away with it.

"You can try, you know," I tell him, already frustrated by the conversation we're about to have. "But I'm not going down without a fight." I ignore the radiating pain I feel from fighting with Mac this morning and drop down into Lindy's vacated rocking chair. "Look, man. I don't know why you're so pissed."

"You've got two sisters, and you don't know why I'm so pissed? What the hell's wrong with you, Sinclair?" He looks at me, equally pissed and baffled, and I'm so fucking over this shit. "Are you really going to sit there, in my fucking rocking chair, on my fucking land, at my fucking house, and blow smoke up my ass?"

I look out over the lake views he's got from both sides of his house.

"It's a nice piece of land. Kinda private. Peaceful," I add as I kick my feet up on the ottoman in front of me, thinking this is what I want—Mackenzie and me and a house full of kids running around, safe from the rest of the world. I want a compound.

"Seriously . . . you were living with Ares Wilder when it came out that he'd been sleeping with Gracie. How do you expect me to believe you didn't want to rip him limb from limb?"

He puts his coffee down and stands from his chair, then walks over to the front door and yanks it open, and Lindy practically topples through it from the inside. "Princess . . . Hasn't anyone ever told you it's not nice to eavesdrop?"

She rolls her eyes, and I stifle a laugh.

"You know you're going to tell me everything later anyway. This way, we don't have to waste time before you have to get on the plane this afternoon."

He wraps his hand around the back of her neck and whispers something I can't hear, and Lindy Hayes giggles before she walks her ass right back inside that house. "Sorry, Nix. I tried," she calls out just before she shuts the door.

"Now." He turns around, crosses his arms, and leans back against the porch railing. "Tell me how happy you were for Gracie and Ares when you found out he knocked her up."

"Listen, man, I'm trying to be patient here. But you talk shit about my sister again, and I'll give you a fucking reason to hate me. We're not so different, you know. I'm a protective bastard too. The difference is, Ares is a good guy who made my sister happy. He's a fucking great dad to my niece and nephew, and my sister fucking loves him. I can see all of that. You just see someone who what—took my sister away? That's fucking sick, she's not mine that way. She's his. She'll always be my sister, but she's his fucking world."

"Am I supposed to believe in what—a few weeks— months, maybe . . . you made her your world?"

Hardheaded fucking pain in the ass.

"How about you ask your sister? Or hey," I push back. "I've only been on your team for four years before this. And you know, your sister and your wife both practically lived at my house growing up. How about you trust me to not be a gigantic fucking disrespectful dick."

"You weren't there, Nixon. You didn't listen to her cry herself to sleep for a year straight. You didn't see the pain she lived through." He shifts as his voice goes from angry to less . . . "Go through that, and then tell me I'm supposed to trust her to anyone else."

"Do you want me to apologize for not going through hell, E? *Sorry.* You happy?" I stand up and move across from him. "Just because I trusted my sister to live her own life and make her own decisions doesn't mean I'm any less protective than you are. But here's the thing. I knew Ares Wilder, and he's a good dude. He loves her. He'd never hurt her, and that's all I can ask for."

"You gonna stand there and tell me you love Kenzie? Is that supposed to be a joke?" Oh yeah. That anger comes back with a vengeance, like he can't believe anyone could ever make her happy or put her first, and now I'm gonna kill him.

I throw Easton back against the wall with a hand to his throat, no longer giving a shit that he's Mac's brother or my goalie.

"Fuck you, man. I asked her to marry me last night. She's going to be my wife, and you can either get on board or get the fuck off the train. But I'm going to marry her. I'm going to love her and protect her. And there's not a goddamn thing you can do to stop me." I rip my hand away from his throat and shove him away. "Get over yourself, man. You take care of your fucking family, and I'll take care of mine."

He looks like he just took a puck to the chest.

"Did she say yes?" he asks quietly. Hurt, if I had to guess.

"Yeah . . ." I smile, unable to be pissed when I think about last night. "She did."

"Fuck . . ." he hisses. "I didn't even know you were together."

"I love her, E. I think I always have. You can hate me all you want. But you better get used to me. Because I'm not going anywhere."

Not if I can get her to talk to me again.

Landed in Calgary. Headed to our rooms now. First game is tomorrow night. We have walk through in the morning.

NIXON

How was your day?

NIXON

Love you, baby. Sleep well.

NIXON

Morning, Mac.

NIXON

Guess who thought Easton and I should room together for this game?

NIXON

If you guessed Jace, you'd be the winner. Your brother says Jace is paying him back for when Easton married Lindy. Apparently, you and I are bringing it full circle.

NIXON

Don't ask me. I have no idea what they're thinking.

NIXON

Okay, so Easton and I now have a common enemy. Jace.

NIXON

We may have put Saran Wrap over his toilet last night.

NIXON

It was Easton's idea.

NIXON

You've got to forgive me, Mac, I can't stand not talking to you.

KENZIE

Forgiving you has nothing to do with being mad at you. I forgive you. But I'm still furious. And when I'm mad, I shut down.

I watched your game on TV with Callen. Nice goal.

J look at the time when we get off the plane after our Calgary game, and board the hotel bus in Alberta. It's too late to call her.

Fuck.

NIXON

Morning, baby. One more game, and then I'm home tonight.

Are you on call?

KENZIE

. . .

No. Not tonight. I'm heading to the hospital for rounds now. I'll be home before your game.

NIXON

Mac . . . You asked me not to shut you out once. I'm asking you now to not shut me out. Shutting down might be how you deal, but fuck, baby, I can't do this.

KENZIE

I'll see you tonight, Nixon. Have a good game.

I guess that's a start.

Kenzie

Chapter 27

Forgiving is easy. Forgetting is hard.
Admitting you may have overreacted is fucking torture.

—Kenzie's Secret Thoughts

"So are you going to forgive him?" Bellamy asks from the other side of the counter while we pay for our dinners in the hospital cafeteria. Not that her brownie and yogurt count for a meal to anyone past the age of eight, but, I'm trying not to judge.

"Nixon or Easton?" I ask as we find a table, rethinking my salad. "I've already forgiven Nixon. I'm just still pissed. He shouldn't have kept it from me."

"Is that really why you're still pissed? Or is it because he called you out on the Dr. Dick thing?" I stab a cucumber with my fork and stare at her brownie. Maybe Bellamy has the right idea.

"I wish he'd told me. But I'm pretty sure I'm more mad at myself for overreacting than I am at him for putting me in the position in the first place. I've just dug my heels in so deep, it's kinda hard to pull them out," I admit, so damn frustrated.

"The first step is admitting you have a problem," she chirps, reminding me a little of Leo. "The second step is the make-up sex. Make-up sex is so much fun."

Huh . . . I hadn't thought about it that way.

"Now, onto Easton. Are you pissed at him too?"

"Maybe give me a little bit more of a transition between hot make-up sex with my fiancé and asking me about my brother," I groan. "But yes. Him, I'm still mad at. I'm a grown woman. You think that dumbass would have a little faith in my decision-making skills."

"What time is your meeting with HR?"

"In an hour," I tell her, knowing I have to do this. I should have done it weeks ago.

She looks between the brownie and yogurt sitting side by side on her tray, then picks up the brownie and hands it to me. "Pretty sure you need this more than I do."

Once I'm home, I shower and change into leggings and Nixon's Boston University hoodie. It's not the new Revolution one he gave me, but this one smells like him, and after the day I've had, I need the comfort.

Gordie and I curl up on the couch, and I open my Kindle, needing a distraction.

Fourteen chapters later, the shifters have rejected each other, then somehow fall in love with each other anyway, and I'm reminded why I love shifter romance.

The Alpha possessiveness is off the charts, and I'm here for it.

We're just about to get to their first time together when my door opens, and my breath catches in my throat. "Nix . . ."

"Hey, baby," he murmurs and crosses the room in two long strides before picking me up and crushing me to him. "Christ, Mac. I missed you so much."

I wrap my legs around his waist, and he sits us both down, and I cling to him. "Me too, Nix." My eyes fill with unshed tears. "It's been awful without you home, and us fighting, and today was such a bad day, and you were the only person I wanted to tell. I'm so sorry. I shouldn't have frozen you out. It would have killed me if you did that to me. I won't do that again—"

"Shh," he cuts me off before pressing his lips to mine. "Slow down and breathe, Mac."

I rest my head against his chest and listen to his heart beat for a few long minutes before opening my mouth again. "I'm sorry I didn't listen to you the other morning. I should have given you a chance to explain, and I didn't. I trust you, Nix. But this is all so damn new and scary. It doesn't make it better, but hopefully, next time, I won't be like this."

He lifts my face to his. "There's not going to be a next time, Mac. I called Hunter and told him to kill any trade talks."

"It won't be our last fight though. We've got to work on better communication." I close my eyes and soak in his warmth. "Don't keep things from me again. Be honest with me from the beginning. I don't need to be protected. Just loved." I smile and take his hand in mine. "Tell me why you wanted the trade."

"I don't even have a good answer anymore. I thought a different city could help me create my own legacy instead of always feeling like I'm just a piece of my father's. I did it to myself. My dad has never made me feel that way. It's me making me feel that way." He pushes my hair over my shoulders and tugs on the hood of my sweatshirt. "My clothes look so fucking good on you, baby. But I have something else for you to try on."

"Oh, don't you worry. I've helped myself to a few things in your closet since you've been gone," I admit sheepishly.

Nixon pulls a tiny red velvet box from his pants pocket and holds it up between us. "I hope you're still willing to give me the same answer, Mackenzie. Tell me I didn't fuck this up beyond repair and you'll still marry me."

He cracks the box open to show me a beautiful brilliant-cut, platinum solitaire, and in typical Nixon fashion, it's gigantic.

"Nixon . . . It's beautiful."

He pulls it from the box and slides it down my finger. "Is that a yes, baby?"

I press my lips to his. "I already told you yes. That never changed. I was pissed. Not done. Never done."

My doorman buzzes my condo.

"Dr. Hayes. Juliette and Becket Kingston are here and coming up."

Certain people have automatic entrée privileges. Jules and Becks are both on that list. I just get a courtesy notification. Thankfully. Because five minutes later, and they might have walked in on something that no parent—biological or surrogate—needs to walk in on.

"Everything okay?" Nixon asks, and I stand from his lap.

"I don't know. I wasn't expecting them." A ball of dread tightens in my stomach.

This isn't normal.

I grab my phone from the table and immediately dial Easton.

"Kenz, are you okay? Did he fuck up already?"

"That's how you answer the phone, E? Really? I'm fine, but Becks and Jules are heading up to my condo at eleven at night, in the middle of the night, without calling. I needed to hear your voice. Everything okay with you?"

"Yeah, but stay on the phone. I want to know what's going on with Becks and Jules."

I slide him to speaker and look at Nix. "I just put you on speaker, and Nixon's here with me, FYI."

"Fuck face," Easton greets Nixon.

"Dickhead," Nixon responds, and I look between my future husband and my brother's name on my screen.

"I guess you guys got over your shit?" I ask both of them as Jules and Becks knock on my door.

"Yup. We both agreed if he hurts you, he dies," Easton answers, and I shake my head and hand Nixon the phone before I answer the door.

"We also agreed Easton's an overbearing asshole who needs to back the fuck off. But I think we're doing dinner at his house Sunday, if you're not working," Nixon adds, and Easton groans.

"I said takeout, man. Lindy can't cook for shit. Don't let her lie to you."

I shake my head and open my door. Becket holds Juliette's hand in his, but they both drop them and wrap their arms around me. "Thank God, you're okay."

The room behind me goes eerily silent.

"I'm fine. What are you talking about?" I ask, utterly confused.

Becket closes the door and ushers Jules and me into the other room, where I move into Nixon's side. "Easton's on speaker phone."

"What the hell is going on?" my brother asks, a scary tone taking over.

"Honey, why don't you sit down," Jules tells me, and the hairs on my arms stand on end.

"Tell me what's going on—now. Is someone dead?" I ask

quietly, scared of the answer, and the look on their faces tells me I'm right. "Who," I cry out, and if it weren't for Nixon's arms, I'd fall to my knees.

"Why didn't you tell us about Dr. Richardson, sweetheart?" Becket asks with so much emotion in his words, it's hard to understand him.

I look from Nixon back to Becks and Jules. "Honestly, I didn't want to worry you. I thought if I ignored it, it would go away. But Nixon helped me realize that wasn't the way to handle it, so I went to HR and reported him today."

"You did?" Nix asks, and I nod hesitantly.

"You were right. I was going to tell you—"

He pulls me against him and buries his face in my hair. "So fucking brave, baby."

He doesn't whisper it. Doesn't care that anyone else can hear him.

"I love you," I tell him as I tighten my hold on his waist.

"Kenzie." The way Becket says my name makes me shake. "Dr. Richardson was put on administrative leave after you registered your complaint today. He went to his house and shot himself."

"Oh my God." For the second time tonight, my knees give out, and Nixon takes all my weight. "I wanted him fired. Not dead."

"This is not your fault, baby." Nixon holds me up as shock and anger course over his face. "You didn't do anything wrong. He did. And if he killed himself over it, he must have done so much more to other women than what he did to you. He was inappropriate, but he never touched you or hurt you . . ."

His words hang thick in the air, as if waiting for me to correct him.

"No. Never. I think he backed off because of you, Nix." I

don't know why I'm crying, but now that the tears have started, they won't stop.

Nixon picks me up and sits me down on the couch, His strong arms holding me together when I feel like I might break. "Is this my fault?" I ask, but then shake my head. "No. *No*. I will not let him make me take this on. I didn't do this."

"You didn't do anything wrong, Kenz." Becket sits next to me and rubs my back as I lean forward trying to calm my breathing. "The police are going to want a statement though."

"I'll take you tomorrow," Nixon tells me, but he's looking over my head at Becket.

A silent understanding passes between them.

"I'm going to make a pot of coffee," Juliette announces as I pull my knees up to my chest. And hours later, when we finally convince them they need to go home and Nixon and I are lying in bed, it all seems like a crazy dream.

"Nix . . ." I drag my nails up and down his arm, unable to lie still.

"Yeah, baby . . ." He hasn't let go of me all night. My strength when I had none left.

"Can we move out of this fucking building?"

"About that . . . I kinda did a thing."

I lean up on his chest and stare into his eyes. "What did you do?"

"I had my business manager cash in my trust fund the other day, and I bought the Cherry Tree Estate off the big lake."

"That's like a hundred acres . . . the farmhouse is massive and there's a ton of other houses on that property besides the old farmhouse." I tell him, like he doesn't already know it. At least, I'm assuming he does, since apparently, he bought it.

"Want to help me redo an old farmhouse?"

"By help you, you mean we hire people, right? Because I operate on bodies for a living. My hands are insured. I don't use construction tools." I press my lips to his chest and bite his nipple. "Didn't think you might have wanted to ask me first?" I tease.

"It was spur of the moment. But if you don't want to live there, we'll fix it up and flip it. No harm, no foul."

"I think it's a great idea, and I might even have one better. Let's have the wedding there."

His hand runs up my back, pressing me tighter. "That sounds like a plan, baby."

"I love you Nixon. Thanks for waiting for me."

"I'd have waited a lifetime for you, Mac. Forever . . ."

"Forever."

**If I did anything right in my life, it was loving you.
Today. Tomorrow. Always.**

—Nixon's Secret Thoughts

"I'd like to make a toast." Dad raises his glass in the air and looks around the room we have set up for the groomsmen to relax in before the wedding starts. "Love isn't always easy, but it's always worth it with the right person. That woman who's going to walk down the aisle in a few minutes has always been the right person for you, son. *Salut.*"

"*Salut,*" the guys echo and turn back to their conversation as Dad fixes my tie. "You're a lucky man to have found her, son. And she's a lucky woman to be loved by you. Since the day you were born, not a day has passed when I haven't been proud of you."

"You cast a big shadow, Dad. And for a long time, I thought that meant I had to fight against it to find my own way. Mac helped me realize that embracing it made me stronger—because being your son is a huge piece of who I am. You lit the way for all of us, then embraced it when we went different ways." I clap his back and lean in. "I hope my kid is as lucky as we were."

Dad's eyes widen.

"Not a word to anyone else, old man," I warn. "Not yet. Not tonight."

"Love you, kid." He shakes my hand and pulls me in for a hug.

"I think we should do shots every time Dad hugs someone tonight," Hendrix announces.

"If you're drunk for pictures, your mother will kill you," Grandpa warns, and Leo takes the glass out of Hendrix's hand.

Everly pops her head in. "It's time, Nixon."

My heart races, and my brothers and I walk down the aisle together, with Callen, Cross, and Ares behind us, and I wait for the love of my life to meet me under our cherry trees.

Kenzie

"*Y*ou look incredible, Kenzie." Easton runs his hands over my bare arms as he stands behind me while I take one last look in the mirror. "Mom would be so proud of you. I hope you know that."

I wipe my eyes for the hundredth time today and nod, unable to form words.

"If he ever—" he starts, and I stop him.

"He won't." He's been offering to kill Nixon for me for nearly a year, and we've somehow found this shorthand. Three words from him and two from me, but they're all that needs to be said. Nixon would never purposefully hurt me, and he shows me that with his whole heart, every day.

"Thanks for letting me walk you down the aisle," Easton manages to say as he hides his emotion behind a cough.

Becket moves in next to Easton and takes my arm in his, dapper as ever in his beautiful black tux. "She asked me first," Becks teases Easton. "She's just letting you hold her other arm so she doesn't have to hear you whine about it forever."

I look at two of the most important men in my life—second only to Nixon and maybe Gordie, if dogs count—and laugh. "If either of you trip me, there'll be hell to pay. Do you hear me?" I tease.

Juliette moves them both away so she can fix my veil. When she's satisfied, she steps back and hands me my bouquet. "Feet first, Kenzie."

"Just like you and Mom," I whisper back and kiss her cheek. "Okay, is it time to get this show on the road? I'm starving."

"You're crazy," Jules laughs.

"Yeah, but it runs in the family." And we wouldn't have it any other way.

The tent set up on the lawn is enormous. Definitely befitting the only *daughter* of Senator Becket Kingston. The band hasn't stopped playing for hours, and the fireworks were just set off over the lake as the girls and I all watched with our husbands from our private dock.

Nixon stands behind me, his arms wrapped around my waist and his lips skimming my ear. "Was it everything you wanted, baby?"

"It was more," I whisper back, completely at peace.

The band announces they're taking a break, and they turn on an old James Bay song I love, and I turn in my husband's arm. "Dance with me."

"For the rest of our lives, baby."

"He still calls her *baby*," Everly fake whispers.

"Bet she likes his dick even more now than she used to too," Lindy adds, and Gracie gasps.

"You can't say that when she's wearing a wedding dress," she hushes us all right before we all burst out laughing, and the guys stare at us like we're crazy. We are. And they should be used to it by now.

"It's a wedding dress, Gracie, not some saintly robe or something. He's going to boink her in it later anyway," Brynnie tells her, and I bury my face in Nixon's chest, knowing what's coming next.

"He better not be boinking my sister," Easton growls, and Lindy cups his cheek.

"Oh, sweetie, don't you worry. She's a virgin bride, and it's an immaculate conception."

Oh shit.

Everyone stops talking all at once, but Easton is the first to speak. "You're pregnant, Kenzie?"

He looks from Nixon to me, his eyes welling with tears.

He's turned into quite the sap since he had kids of his own.

I nod and squeeze Nixon's hand. "We weren't going to tell anyone tonight."

"Why the hell did Lindy know?" Everly asks, and I just shake my head.

"Because someone needed to make sure it looked like I was drinking even though I wasn't." I wink at Lindy. "Nothing says knocked-up bride quite like her not taking part in the champagne toast."

Nixon beams with pride. "I would have taken out an ad in the *Kroydon Kronicles* if she let me. I can't wait."

"God, I love you." I press my lips to his and hum deep in my throat as he grabs my ass through about a dozen layers of Italian silk.

"Seriously, stop," Easton groans. "I can't unsee that."

"You better look away then." Nix grabs my ass in both hands and walks away with me. "I've been good all day, Mrs. Sinclair. I think it's about time I get my reward."

"Oh, Mr. Sinclair, I think we have one more lesson to go." I ignore the clapping as he carries me into the centuries-old farmhouse we've had completely restored to its earlier glory.

"Oh yeah, baby. What lesson is that?" he teases, taking the stairs two at a time.

I bite down on his earlobe and tug. "I'm going to need you to show me how you fuck your wife."

"That might be my favorite lesson yet." He tosses me onto our bed, and the layers of silk puff up around me like a cloud.

"Don't worry. We'll come up with another one tomorrow," I promise.

"So many tomorrows, baby."

"So many lessons still to come, Nix."

The End

Want more Kenzie & Nixon?
Download their extended epilogue!

Download the bonus epilogue here

The Philly Press

NOT READY TO SAY GOODBYE YET?

Are you ready to see which of Kroydon Hills men falls next?

There's plenty of secrets they've been keeping from you and you're not going to believe what they are.

Make sure to preorder *Redeeming,* book 2 in *Red Lips & White Lies,* to see what secrets Callen's been keeping…

Preorder Redeeming Now

#KroydonKronicles #Redeeming

If you haven't read the first book in the Kings Of Kroydon Hills series, you can start with *All In* today!

Read All In for FREE on KU

ACKNOWLEDGMENTS

Thank you so much to my family for all of your support. My husband and children are my world and my time with them often gets sacrificed for my time with these characters.

Thank you to my amazing team. I cannot imagine doing this without each and every one of you. Dena, Callie, Jen, Tammy, Kelly, Vicki, Morgan, Valentine, Val and Shannon - I have no words big enough to show my appreciation.

And to my incredible momager, Bri. One more down and an infinite number of books still to go. Thank you for managing my business and my life.

As always, my biggest thanks goes to you, the reader, for taking a chance on Nixon & Kenzie, and this fictional town I love so much. I hope you enjoyed reading Tempting as much as I've enjoyed writing it.

ABOUT THE AUTHOR

Bella Matthews is a USA Today & Amazon Top 5 Bestselling author. She is married to her very own Alpha Male and raising three little ones. You can typically find her running from one sporting event to another. When she is home, she is usually hiding in her home office with the only other female in her house, her rescue dog Tinker Bell by her side. She likes to write swoon-worthy heroes and sassy, smart heroines. Sarcasm is her love language and big family dynamics are her favorite thing to add to each story.

Stay Connected

Amazon Author Page: https://amzn.to/2UWU7Xs
Facebook Page: https://www.facebook.com/Bella.
Matthews.Author
Reader Group: https://www.facebook.com/groups/
bellamatthewsgamechangers
Instagram: https://www.instagram.com/bellamatthews.
author/
Bookbub: https://bit.ly/BMBookbub
Goodreads: https://bit.ly/BMGoodreads
TikTok: http://tiktok.com/@bellamatthewsauthor
Newsletter: https://bit.ly/BMNLsingups
Patreon: https://www.patreon.com/BellaMatthews

ALSO BY BELLA MATTHEWS

Kings of Kroydon Hills

All In

More Than A Game

Always Earned, Never Given

Under Pressure

Restless Kings

Rise of the King

Broken King

Fallen King

The Risks We Take Duet

Worth The Risk

Worth The Fight

Defiant Kings

Caged

Shaken

Iced

Overruled

Haven

Playing To Win

The Keeper

The Wildcat

The Knockout

The Sweet Spot

Red Lips & White Lies

Tempting

Redeeming

Enticing

Captivating

Teasing

CHECK OUT BELLA'S WEBSITE

Scan the QR code or go to http://authorbellamatthews.com
to stay up to date with all things Bella Matthews

Made in United States
Troutdale, OR
11/11/2024

24645120R00170